MW00626679

WHAT SHE DID

A DETECTIVE CHARLOTTE PIERCE NOVEL

KATE GABLE

BYRD BOOKS

COPYRIGHT

Proofreaders:

Julie Deaton, Deaton Author Services, https://www.facebook.com/jdproofs/

Renee Waring, Guardian Proofreading Services, https://www.facebook.com/GuardianProofreadingServices

Cover Design: Kate Gable

Visit my website at www.kategable.com

BE THE FIRST TO KNOW ABOUT MY UPCOMING SALES, NEW RELEASES AND EXCLUSIVE GIVEAWAYS!

Want a Free book? Sign up for my Newsletter!

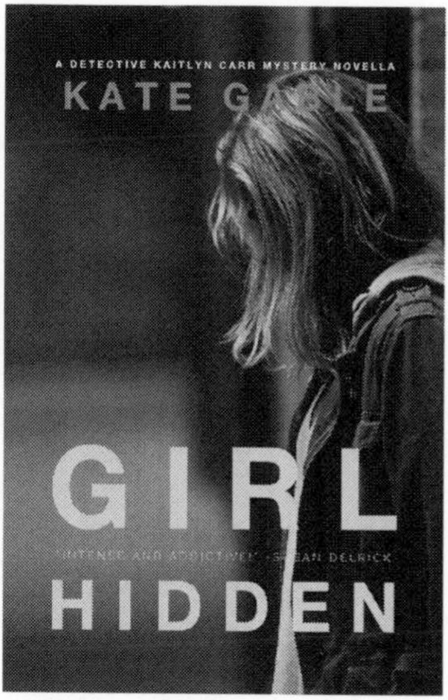

Sign up for my newsletter:
https://www.subscribepage.com/kategableviplist

Join my Facebook Group:
https://www.facebook.com/groups/833851020557518

Bonus Points: Follow me on BookBub and Goodreads!

https://www.goodreads.com/author/show/21534224.Kate_Gable

ABOUT KATE GABLE

Kate Gable loves a good mystery that is full of suspense. She grew up devouring psychological thrillers and crime novels as well as movies, tv shows and true crime.

Her favorite stories are the ones that are centered on families with lots of secrets and lies as well as many twists and turns. Her novels have elements of psychological suspense, thriller, mystery and romance.

Kate Gable lives near Palm Springs, CA with her husband, son, a dog and a cat. She has spent more than twenty years in Southern California and finds inspiration from its cities, canyons, deserts, and small mountain towns.

She graduated from University of Southern California with a Bachelor's degree in Mathematics. After pursuing graduate studies in mathematics, she switched gears and got her MA in Creative Writing and English from Western New Mexico University and her PhD in Education from Old Dominion University.

Writing has always been her passion and obsession. Kate is also a USA Today Bestselling author of romantic suspense under another pen name.

Write her here:

Kate@kategable.com

Check out her books here:

www.kategable.com

Sign up for my newsletter:
https://www.subscribepage.com/kategableviplist

Join my Facebook Group:
https://www.facebook.com/groups/833851020557518

Bonus Points: Follow me on BookBub and Goodreads!

https://www.bookbub.com/authors/kate-gable

https://www.goodreads.com/author/show/21534224.Kate_Gable

amazon.com/Kate-Gable/e/B095XFCLL7
facebook.com/kategablebooks
bookbub.com/authors/kate-gable
instagram.com/kategablebooks

ALSO BY KATE GABLE

All books are available at ALL major retailers! If you can't find it, please email me at **kate@kategable.com**

Detective Kaitlyn Carr

Girl Missing (Book 1) - FREE for a Limited Time!

Girl Lost (Book 2)
Girl Found (Book 3)
Girl Taken (Book 4)
Girl Forgotten (Book 5)
Girl Hidden (FREE Novella)

Detective Charlotte Pierce
What She Did
When She Left
How She Disappeared

ABOUT WHAT SHE DID

☆☆☆☆☆ *"Gripping! Fascinating mystery thriller filled with intriguing characters and lots of twists and turns!" (Goodreads)*

She walks through the strangely familiar house, hardwood floors creaking under her feet. ***They* are in bed:** peaceful, except for the **pool of blood** spreading across the white sheets.

A couple expecting their first child is brutally murdered in their home. The prime suspect? The scorned ex-wife who supposedly has no knowledge of why she's there or what happened.

When Detective Charlotte Pierce arrives at the scene, it's up to her to unravel the mystery of newlyweds' murder. It looks like an open and shut case, but certain things are not adding up.

Despite pressures from her FBI director father, Charlotte came to Mesquite County to escape the burdens of a big city police department. She has been through a lot and a quiet suburban community where nothing really happens is exactly what she is looking for.

Little does she know that this quiet community is filled with secrets of its own, including those within the police department. She could easily go with the flow, but she refuses to ignore even the smallest inconsistencies.

Was it the ex-wife or is the murderer still out there?

Can Charlotte get to the truth before he kills again?

This suspenseful thriller is perfect for fans of James Patterson, Leslie Wolfe, Lisa Regan, L. T. Vargus and Karin Slaughter. It has mystery, angst, a bit of romance and family drama.

Praise for Kate Gable's Girl Missing Series

☆☆☆☆☆"Gripping! This book was a great read. I found a new author that I enjoy and I can't wait to read the rest of the series! " *(Goodreads)*

☆☆☆☆☆ "The twists come at you at breakneck pace. Very suspenseful." *(Goodreads)*

☆☆☆☆☆ "I really enjoyed the ins and outs of the storyline, it kept me reading so that I could find out how the story would turn out. And the ending was a major shocker, I never saw it coming. I truly recommend this book to everyone who loves mysteries and detective stories." *(Goodreads)*

☆☆☆☆☆" I loved it. One of the best books I've ever read." - Amazon review

☆☆☆☆☆ "I couldn't put the book down I give it a thumbs up and I would recommend it to other readers" *(Goodreads)*

☆☆☆☆☆ "Another great book in the Kaitlyn Carr series! I am so drawn into these books. I love that they are not just about Kaitlyn's search for her sister but also about a case she is working on. I can't wait for the final book in the series!" *(Goodreads)*

1

ERIN

Something bad is about to happen. Goose bumps run down my spine. I step on the accelerator to get there faster.

I don't know where I'm going. Rain is falling sideways in sheets.

A sappy love song program, easy listening for the over thirties, comes to a close. It must be after midnight.

How does that saying go again? Nothing good happens this late at night.

I pull onto a familiar looking street.

I don't think I've ever been here before, but it's familiar in that way that all planned communities are.

Perfectly spaced trees. Immaculate lawns. Pristine roofs. Houses painted the same three colors.

I turn right onto a cul-de-sac.

Wait a second, I think I've been here before.

Three black mailboxes in a row.

The BMW SUV parked at the house next door.

The rose bushes right under the white shutters.

This house is different. It's a little unlike all the others.

Parking in the front, I get out of the car.

The rain that has sent my windshield wipers into overdrive, somehow catches me by surprise. The droplets hit me like little pins.

I should feel cold, but I don't feel anything.

My gaze follows the water down to the ground.

Crouching down, I knock off a few raindrops from a blade of grass. It vibrates like a violin string.

Getting up, I head up the steps. I run my finger over the glass window and peek inside.

You know it's a safe neighborhood where nothing ever happens when there's glass surrounding the front door for anyone to peek through.

My index finger meanders over to the button.

Soft and rounded, it invites me to press it. But it would be rude to use the doorbell in the middle of the night.

My other hand presses down on the door handle.

Much to my surprise, the door opens.

I take a deep breath and step inside.

I walk through an unfamiliar living room. The hardwood floor creaks underneath my footsteps.

It's dark, but the room is illuminated by the city lights streaming in through the cathedral windows.

I look around.

It's a modern, relatively newly constructed home, much like my own.

But the ceilings are much higher, well over twelve feet.

To my left is an elegant formal dining room, which is probably only used on holidays and other special occasions.

The open floorplan winds around, leading me to the kitchen with stainless steel appliances and crown molding to complete the look.

The cabinets are light and the waterfall countertop island is huge with seating for at least five.

"Where am I?" I whisper to myself.

As I make my way down the hallway, I suddenly stop dead in my tracks.

No.

It can't be.

I pick up one of the framed pictures from the side table and look at their smiling faces.

There's Susannah with her long, elegant legs. Derek is kneeling down next to her with his arms around her stomach.

I can almost smell the grass and the sunflowers behind them. This is their pregnancy photo shoot.

I put down this photo and pick up another.

It's Derek and Susannah lying on a beach.

I read the word *Jamaica* on the frame and double over to catch myself from throwing up.

The room fades to black. When my vision comes back, it's blurry and full of spots.

Rising to my feet, my head starts to throb. The ache pounds so hard that all I hear is the sound of blood rushing in between my ears.

Somewhere in the distance, something catches my eye.

I squint, trying to focus.

The French doors at the end of the hallway are wide open.

Walking over, I trip over my own feet and grab onto the wall to keep myself upright.

There, in the distance, against the wall, in the king-sized bed, I see *them*.

My stomach ties up in a knot. A familiar queasy feeling rises up my body to the back of my throat.

They're just asleep, I say to myself. They're just asleep.

Blood runs cold through my veins.

My heart jumps into my chest.

I take a few steps back, slipping on the puddle of something viscous.

When I lift up my foot, I see the dark liquid all over the bottom of my slip-on shoes.

Blood.

Oh my God.

I stepped in the blood.

I look at the couple lying in the bed. Neither of them makes a sound.

Please get up and kick me out of your house, I plead silently.

Neither of them moves a muscle.

I take a deep breath.

I can't just walk out.

This is Derek's house and that's Derek and Susannah in bed.

And if they aren't asleep…I let my thoughts trail off, unable to follow through with the rest of the sentence.

There's only one thing to do.

I take another deep breath and walk through the doors into the master bedroom on my tiptoes, holding my breath.

"Wake up," I say. "Please wake up."

I should yell at the top of my lungs, but I'm terrified.

I can barely make my voice go louder than a whisper.

They are just sleeping, I say to myself.

When I reach the end of the sprawling bed, I see Susannah's long hair spread out on the pillow. Her face is facing away from me.

I watch her body and wait for her chest to move up and down with her breath. But nothing happens. The sheet wrapped around her body is drenched in blood.

Derek faces away from me. He's motionless.

"Susannah," I whisper. "Don't be dead."

You can't be dead, I say to myself over and over.

Carefully, I place my hand on her shoulder. Her arm falls off his side. The weight of it pulls her body from the bed and onto the floor.

Something within me shifts.

"Susannah! Susannah!" I yell, kneeling down and grabbing her by the shoulders.

I shake her as hard as I can. But her head just bops from side to side as if independent from the rest of her.

Her body is limp, missing all signs of life. My hand lands in some gooey substance that's covering her lower half. Black and viscous, it doesn't seem like blood at all.

Repulsed, I'm also mesmerized, unable to stop staring at my open-faced palm.

A moment later, when I finally come to my senses, I walk around the bed to Derek's side.

He always had to have the left-hand side of the bed. No matter whether we were in our own house or a hotel room.

And here he is, lying on the left-hand side of Susannah, shot in the head.

Looking at little dark particles splattered all over his white puffy pillow, this place feels like a scene in a play.

Or maybe it's just a dream…

Wasn't this something I had secretly wished for over this past year?

Taking a step backward, my foot starts to slide.

Before I know what's really happening, my legs fly in the air and the rest of me hurls toward the floor.

I land flat on my back.

My chest seizes up and I can't take in a breath.

A few moments pass as I struggle to inhale and finally manage to get some air.

Turning to one side, I prop myself up on my elbow to get up.

Then I slip again.

I can feel the cold, wet blood sticking to my back and the side of my body. I am covered in their death.

Before I can scramble up to my feet, I feel sick to my stomach. A big lump makes its way up my body and I throw up all over the floor.

2

ERIN

Derek and Susannah are gone. Dead. Despite what I may or may not have thought earlier, this is definitely not a dream. I wash my mouth out in their kitchen sink.

But how?

And why?

My shirt, covered in blood, is sticking to my back. It's making me feel even colder than I already am.

I wrap my arms around my shoulders and try to remember if I had left my coat anywhere.

Or even if I had it with me at all. I want to take off this wet, dirty shirt, but going back there to look to change into something of Derek's, or Susannah's, is out of the question.

What do I do now?

I debate whether I can just leave. Maybe, I can pretend that I was never here. But then the blood soaked shirt presses against my bare skin. Looking down, I see my bloody footprints all over their hardwood floors.

No, I don't have a choice.

They're going to find out anyway. I have to be the one to make the call.

The police arrive quickly.

The first officer on the scene is a large, burly man with a thick mustache who walks through the house with an overblown sense of authority.

He asks me a couple of questions, but mostly just walks around the primary bedroom making sure that they are in fact dead.

The paramedics arrive at about the same time and everyone gets busy doing their own thing; measuring something, marking other things, looking for evidence and then, when they find it, placing it in plastic bags.

Having done my part by reporting the murder, I look around for a place to sit but don't want to get anything dirty.

"Ms. Lowry?" A woman with a no-nonsense attitude walks up to me. I look at her. "Or do you prefer Bryson?"

Bryson is Derek's last name. It's Susannah's name, too.

"I'm back to Lowry now," I say.

"Ms. Lowry, my name is Detective Pierce."

She doesn't give me her first name. Is this the way that she normally introduces herself or does she just not want me to know?

The paramedics have given me a gray blanket and I wrap it tightly around myself.

Detective Pierce is dressed in a leather jacket and is holding a cup of coffee. She's fit, with light brown shoulder-length hair and wide eyes. She isn't beautiful in that drop-dead gorgeous way that police officers are depicted on television but there is something striking about her.

"Can I ask you a few questions?" she asks, sitting down next to me.

I nod.

"You were the one who called this in. Is that correct?"

I nod again.

"Can you tell me what you found?"

I go over everything that happened.

Walking through the house. Seeing the blood on the floor. Walking into the bedroom.

Trying to revive Susannah. Her falling onto the floor. Slipping and falling in her blood.

Throwing up.

The words sound ridiculous coming out of my mouth, but I try to report the truth as accurately as possible.

"Okay," Detective Pierce says, nodding her head after I finish my story. "And what were you doing here, Ms. Lowry?"

This question hits me as if it were a baseball bat.

What was I doing here? I have no idea.

I search my mind for the answer, but come up short.

The last thing I remember is walking through the house.

"Ms. Lowry?" Detective Pierce asks, leaning so close to me that I can smell coffee on her breath.

"You can call me Erin," I say quietly, trying to buy some time and hoping that I can come up with some kind of reasonable explanation.

Her question should not have taken me by surprise and yet…it did.

"Why were you here?" Detective Pierce asks.

"I have no idea," I say after a moment. "The last thing I remember is just walking through the house and seeing the blood and going into their room."

Detective Pierce furrows her brow.

She's skeptical, unable or unwilling to believe me. Why would she? My story is…implausible.

My head starts to throb and my mouth is parched again. I clear my throat, hoping to make the dryness go away, but end up coughing instead.

"And why are you covered in blood?" she asks after a moment.

I stare at her.

"I just told you," I say. "I slipped and fell."

"When you first saw the bodies, where were they?"

"What do you mean?"

"Did you disturb anything?"

"Just when I was trying to see if Susannah was okay," I say. "She…fell off the bed."

I just went over all of this. Why is she asking me again?

Detective Pierce writes something down in her little notebook. She must've had it out but I don't remember seeing it before.

"I already told you all of this," I say. "And I already told that officer all of this as well."

"Ms. Lowry, please calm down," she says without looking up from her notebook.

"You are insinuating that I did something that I didn't do," I protest.

"I am not insinuating anything. I am just asking questions," she says, starting to walk away. "Please wait here."

I exhale deeply when she leaves. A feeling of tiredness sweeps over me. It takes all of my strength just to keep my eyes open.

"Ms. Lowry?" someone says, putting their arm on my shoulder. I shudder awake.

"We need your clothes for evidence," the young woman, dressed in scrubs, says.

She hands me some clothing and leads me to the powder room down the hall with a white marble vanity and modern brass fixtures.

Finally, I can take off this blood stained shirt. I wait for her to leave, but she says that's against protocol. She does give me the courtesy of turning around.

I'm relieved as I climb into the baggy Mesquite County Sheriff's Department sweatpants and an even baggier t-shirt and hoodie. I hand her my clothes and watch her put them into a large evidence bag.

"You put your undergarments in here, too, right?" she asks. I stare at her.

"Your bra and underwear?"

"Oh, no. I didn't know I had to."

"We have to take everything, Ms. Lowry. I'm sorry, I should've made that clearer."

"So, I'm just supposed to not wear anything underneath…" I let my words trail off.

"Yes, please," she says, turning a bit away from me to give me a speck of privacy.

I take off everything and get re-dressed into my state issued sweats. She carefully puts them into separate evidence bags, seals them, and writes something on the front.

After putting on the plastic issued shoes, with one size supposedly fitting all, I make my way back to the modern farmhouse living room. This house is newer and bigger than the one Derek and I purchased and in a newer and fancier neighborhood.

Most of the homes around here cost over a million and have more than four bedrooms just like theirs.

Of all the places to move to, it still irks me that they decided to buy a house here, less than a mile away from where we lived together.

Suddenly, I catch myself.

What are you doing? Their lifeless bodies are lying in the next room!

"Ms. Lowry?" Detective Pierce walks up to me. "I mean, Erin. We are going to have to take you to the station."

"What? Why?"

"There are a few more questions we have to ask you."

"Ask me here."

Detective Pierce shakes her head. "I'm sorry, but we really do have to go to the station."

I nod as my heart sinks into the pit of my stomach.

3

ERIN

At the police station, everything looks and smells like a big box store of stationery supplies and workplace furniture.

There are no visible cells or bars or handcuffs.

It's just a regular office with ordinary employees except that people type using only two fingers on outdated computers.

I'm not under arrest, but I'm not exactly free to go.

They need to have a chat with me, Detective Pierce says, as if we didn't have a chat already.

After three cups of coffee and a sunrise peeking through the blinds, the gravity of my predicament is a bit more clear than it was earlier.

Here is the problem, I was the one who found them. I'm the ex-wife. I know that I look guilty.

I'm their first and primary suspect until they find someone with a better motive.

But for now they're being nice, accommodating because they are trying to get more information.

They are trying to trip me up.

As a lapsed attorney, I know that cops are not to be trusted.

The good ones will do anything to close a case. The bad ones will frame you without a second thought.

I'm supposed to be presumed innocent, but the cops aren't the jury.

Their job is to find out who did it according to the evidence that they have and make their case to the prosecutor.

Detective Pierce has to convince the district attorney that the person she thinks did it actually did do it so that the DA can go confidently in the direction of putting forth a prosecution. DAs don't like to lose so they will not go forward with any case they don't think they can win.

Detective Pierce shows me into a small, windowless room without a speck of character.

There isn't one thing on any of the four walls.

Not a poster, not a picture, not even a two-way mirror. There isn't anything identifying this place as anything but a police station interrogation room.

I take the chair that's nearest to the door, but she asks me to move to the other one across the table.

When I glance at the ceiling, I see a camera pointed right at me.

Even though I know that she brought me here to take my statement, there's a very big difference between knowing and seeing.

I stare at the camera and shivers run down my spine.

"Don't worry about that," Detective Pierce says in her friendliest voice.

"So, you're not recording me?" I challenge her.

The fluorescent lights above our heads make the dark circles under her eyes more pronounced.

Her eyelashes are full and dark, accentuated by mascara.

The confidence that she exudes does not stem from how beautiful she is, but rather by something deep within her.

"I didn't say that," she says.

"Why am I here?" I ask.

She narrows her eyes and takes a deep breath.

"You found your ex-husband dead. You were in his house in the middle of the night. We need your statement."

During my brief stint as a lawyer, I spent my days shuffling estate-planning paperwork as a junior associate. I've never even had a significant conversation with a cop before tonight.

But over the past two years, I have consumed my share of crime programming. True crime investigative reports. Netflix documentaries. Cable television shows. You name it, I've probably seen it. Being unemployed and depressed will do that to you.

What did I learn? Police officers are notorious liars. Their job is to say and do anything to elicit a confession.

"Listen, Ms. Lowry…Erin. I just want to get your side," Detective Pierce says again.

"I already told you what happened. Twice."

"I know, but some things still don't seem to add up."

I stare at her and wait.

"What were you doing at their house in the first place?"

"I don't know," I say, shaking my head. "That's the truth. I don't have the faintest idea."

"Did Derek ask you to come over?"

I shrug.

"What were you doing right before you got there?"

"I don't know."

"Were you out with Derek earlier?"

I shrug again, but then shake my head. "No."

"How do you know if you don't remember?"

"Okay, you're right," I admit, "I don't know. But I don't think so."

"I'm trying to help you here, Erin."

Now, this makes me mad.

"Help me? Help me with what, exactly?"

"You found the bodies. You are the scorned ex-wife. You have no idea what you were doing there. If you don't want to be our primary suspect…you have to give me something else to go on."

I stare at her.

This is a threat.

"I'm not a *scorned* ex-wife," I correct her. "I'm just the ex-wife."

She's trying to get a rise out of me.

"Listen, Erin," her voice suddenly softens and she puts her hand on mine, "I know that you went through a bad divorce. I've had my share of bad relationships. So,

I totally get the impulse to want to do something to your ex. Or the woman he left you for."

She's trying to connect with me, pretending to be my friend. Everything she's saying is a lie for all I know.

"Listen, Detective Pierce. I have no idea what you're talking about. I don't have any ill will toward my ex or his wife. I found them like that and that's why I called you. Do you think I would've called you if I did that to them?"

She sits back in her chair, tapping her fingers on the table.

"How do you explain your presence there?" She tries again.

Suddenly, I've had enough.

"I don't have anything else to say. I'm just going to sit here and wait for my attorney."

I called Sandra on the drive over here. Nothing good happens once they take you to the station and I knew that I would need backup.

Detective Pierce, whose first name I still don't know, leaves the room with a dissatisfied look on her face.

She's probably going to kick herself for not building up a good rapport with me first or for pushing me into a confession too hard, too quickly.

But none of those things would've mattered.

I'm an ex-attorney who watches way too many crime shows.

The only way I would confess to something I haven't done is if I were under the influence or with a gun to my head.

A few minutes later, the door opens and a man with his face buried in a file enters.

Our eyes meet.

We recognize each other immediately.

He raises his eyebrows and suddenly he looks exactly like the man I knew when I was twenty.

"What are you doing here?" I whisper.

4

WILL

I didn't make it to the scene of the double homicide and Charlotte only just caught me up on the case.

The interviewee is the ex-wife of the dead husband and his new wife. She found them in their house and she has no explanation as to what she was doing there.

The fact that the woman called the police seemed like it was going to be an open and shut case.

She did something she regrets.

She thought she could get out of it by telling us the majority of what happened, without actually admitting the fact that she had killed them.

When it comes to interrogations, that's typically how it goes. The suspects admit things up to a point. We, as the detectives and the investigators, have to push them to tell us the whole truth.

Charlotte is usually the closer in these circumstances.

I'm the bad cop, she's the good cop.

But occasionally, when the person of interest is a woman, I play the part of the understanding male.

Grabbing the handle of the interrogation room, I don't expect the job to take more than a few hours.

It has been a long night and she has been through a lot.

She has asked for a lawyer, but that doesn't mean that she won't get things off her chest before he arrives.

In order to get the confession, I have to be nice but efficient.

And above all, I have to be kind and understanding.

Charlotte has already tried to play the bad cop, at least to some degree, and spooked her into asking for counsel.

I won't make the same mistake.

I open the door and freeze. Our eyes meet and my body tenses up and becomes immobile.

I am unable to inhale or exhale until I hear her say my name. I quickly shut the door behind me and put the file on the table.

"What are *you* doing here?" Erin asks, sitting forward in her chair.

For a moment, I think that there must be some mistake.

Maybe she came here looking for me and they put her into this room instead. But then my eyes see the name on top of the file.

I saw that the last name was Lowry, but I didn't make the connection.

How could I?

What are the chances that it would be *her*?

She takes a deep breath, exhaling slowly. The twenty-year-old that I used to know is all but gone.

The woman who sits before me now looks like she hasn't slept in days and is carrying the weight of the world on her shoulders.

"I'm Detective William Torch," I say, extending my hand to hers. She looks puzzled, not quite sure why I'm introducing myself.

The truth is that I'm not sure either.

As soon as we're done here, I have to go back to Charlotte and tell her that I have a conflict of interest.

That this is my old girlfriend, the woman that I told her about.

That would be the right thing to do.

Luckily, Erin follows my lead and shakes my hand.

I glance over at the camera that's pointed directly at her. If I had gotten to the station sooner, then I would've been in that other room from which Charlotte is watching right now.

Erin's attorney will be here soon and I can almost sense her waiting anxiously for me to begin the questioning.

"Can you tell me what happened when you got there?" I start.

"Seriously?" Erin asks.

"Excuse me?"

"Didn't she catch you up on all of this? I mean, I told my story like a million times already. Don't you all share notes?"

"Yes, we do, of course."

"So, let's just fast forward to what you are here to ask me then," she says.

"Fine, let's do that," I say, opening the file. "You said that you were walking through your ex-husband's house and you saw a pool of blood and that's what led you to the bedroom?"

Erin pauses, narrowing her eyes.

I take a deep breath.

Usually, this is one of the most exciting parts of my job. Sitting here, across from the suspect, asking them questions which I know will trip them up in their story. Catching them lying is almost as satisfying as catching them after a long car chase.

But it's not today.

I don't want to know the truth about what happened.

The only thing I want is to be back on my boat with her in my arms talking about spending the rest of our lives together.

"I didn't see any blood at first. I just saw the open doors and I walked over there," she corrects me.

I know immediately that she will be a difficult person to catch in a lie, even if I were earnestly trying.

I look over the file that I had reviewed earlier. What can I ask her that would look like I'm actually trying to find out the truth without risking her telling me the truth?

"What can you tell me about what you were doing last night?"

"Listen, I already told Detective Pierce that I have no idea what I was doing at their house. I just remember walking up to their front door..."

"Did you drive there?"

She thinks about that for a moment and doesn't reply.

I already know that she did. We have her car in police impound, checking it for evidence.

"Yes, I guess so," she confirms. "I don't know how else I could've gotten there."

God, don't say anything else, Erin, I pray silently to myself.

I know that what I'm doing is wrong but I can't let her tell me the truth. Not with the cameras pointed at her, recording every moment.

If she does, then I'll be forced to arrest her right here and now.

"Look, I know my rights. I already asked for my attorney. Where is she?"

"She's on her way," I say.

"That's not good enough."

"I'm sorry about that," I say, erasing the tinge of a smile that pops up at the corners of my lips.

"Well, how about this then? I'm not going to say another word until she gets here."

Technically, Erin is free to go unless we have something to hold her on, but I can't tell her this.

"I'm sorry to hear that," I say, taking the file and leaving the room.

"What was that?" Charlotte roars in my face as soon as I step into the hallway.

"What?" I shrug.

"I have seen you interrogate them and this was…abysmal!"

"I'm sorry that you feel that way, but she's pretty smart. I don't think she's going to tell us anything else."

"She won't unless you try harder."

"I tried hard," I lie. "As did you."

"You know what, Torch," she says, furrowing her brow in anger. "If you weren't up to this, you should've had the balls to tell me. I thought you were going to help."

I'm tempted to match her anger with mine, but I decide on another approach instead.

"I did my best, Charlotte. Not everyone caves."

She's about to say something else, but instead she walks away almost stomping her feet. She's pissed because she knows that I can do a lot better. We both do. What she doesn't know is that I couldn't bring myself to even try.

5

ERIN

Will is trying to help me. The realization dawns on me as soon as he introduces himself as Detective William Torch.

Is that what he's doing now?

Is this really his job? If so, why is he pretending he doesn't know me? Doesn't he want to keep it after all of this is over?

These thoughts and about a hundred others whiz through my mind on the way to yet another administrative process.

Sandra is still not here and, after Will leaves, a uniformed officer comes in and takes me to another room. She tells me that they need to check my body for marks and to photograph me.

Apparently, they were supposed to do this earlier, at the crime scene, when they took my clothes but the tech messed up.

I don't know if consent is necessary in something like this, but it doesn't feel like I have much of an option.

"Can't we just wait until after my lawyer arrives?" I ask.

"Why? Do you have something to hide?" she asks, tilting her head and pulling the camera away from me.

The thing is that I don't. I have nothing to hide. I did nothing wrong. So, perhaps acting like I did isn't in my best interest.

"Can I talk to someone? Detective Torch? Pierce?"

"I'm doing this at their request," the police officer says.

Folding her hands across her body, she looks me up and down and adds, "Are you going to let me do this or not?"

I take a deep breath. The sooner that they can clear me, the sooner they can try to find someone else. So, maybe fighting her on this isn't in my best interest?

I take off the top they issued me earlier. She points to the pants and I pull them off over my shoes.

She looks me over up and down, leaning in closer to get a better look at any markings. There's a small black and blue mark on my upper thigh from where I walked into my dining room table. I'm not sure when it happened because I'm pretty clumsy and my body bruises easily.

I explain what happened, but she just shrugs and continues to snap the camera. Each flicker of the flash is an assault.

She takes about a zillion pictures of it from different angles. Luckily, the bruise has developed quite a lot so I'm pretty sure that an expert can tell them that it didn't happen last night. At least, I hope so. I *really* hope so.

"Okay, I will now collect gunshot residue from your hands," she says, putting the camera on the bathroom sink, next to the soap dispenser.

There's a small puddle of water right nearby and I wait for it to inch its way toward the camera.

But it doesn't.

It just pools nearby, a safe distance away. Is it normal to fixate on small, almost ridiculous details like this during a particularly high stress situation? I don't know if that is the case for everyone, but it has always been for me.

When I was in seventh grade, I got caught stealing lipstick from the local department store. I'd done it already four times with friends, but that time I was alone.

I didn't really need it.

I had the money to buy it, but I did it for the rush that it sent pulsating through my body.

Unfortunately, that time, the associate in *Beds and Bedding* saw me and took me back to the little room to wait for my mom to be called.

The rent-a-cop threatened to call the real police and have me arrested.

As we sat there waiting for my mom to show up, I watched the way his wedding ring dug into his big sausage finger while he typed my information into the computer.

I can still remember how tight the ring looked as he banged on the keyboard just using his index fingers.

"Gunshot residue test?" I ask, clearing my throat. "What's that?"

I have a faint idea of what it is from scant knowledge gleaned from crime shows, but I need her to tell me more.

"Whenever a firearm is discharged, it leaves residue on the shooter's hands and clothes."

Firearm, what a strange word.

Why do law enforcement people insist on using this word instead of 'gun,' like the rest of us? Does it mean something different?

"What kind of residue?" I ask.

"Burnt and unburnt particles from the propellant, the explosive primer. It may also contain fragments of the cartridge case and the bullet."

"So, you think I have that on me?"

"It's policy to test everyone who is at the scene," she says, thinking about it for a moment.

Her other answers come so quickly, methodically, like she has asked them a hundred times before. But *not* this one.

"It's important for us to test the clothing and the skin of possible suspects to determine if they were near a firearm when it was discharged," she repeats herself.

I wait as she washes her hands and her wrists in the sink, dries them, and puts on a new pair of plastic gloves.

Then she looks at my hands again, showing me how to show them to her with hers. I stretch them out and wait.

"I'm visually examining your hands and wrists so that I can record the position of any visible gunshot residue deposits," she explains.

"Residue deposits?" I ask as she takes pictures of my hands.

"Black smudges."

I look down and don't see any black smudges. Except for one tiny one at the bottom of my palm.

But that's nothing. Right? Of course, it's nothing.

"Okay, I'm going to touch you now," she says.

I nod, giving her permission that she clearly does not need.

Holding my left arm above the wrist, she tells me to relax and flex my hand.

I do as she says.

Careful not to touch the sticky surface of the adhesive, she places it across the wrinkled areas of my hand, around the knuckles and palm.

So, this is it? I think to myself, biting my tongue to not ask this out loud.

The name of the test makes it sound so highfalutin and fancy, but, in reality, it's hardly anything beyond a piece of Scotch tape being pressed against my hands.

"What can you typically find out from this test?" I ask.

"Depends on the sample."

"Of course. But in general?"

"Well, the deposits are a result of gasses or particles escaping through openings in the weapon. So, the actual amount of residue on the hands varies with the type of weapon, ammunition, and conditions of discharge."

I nod along, but instead of focusing on the potential gunshot residue that she's collecting, my thoughts drift back to her language.

What is it with cops and this type of formal speaking style? Instead of car, it's a vehicle.

Instead of a gun, it's a firearm.

Instead of a bullet, it's ammunition.

Is this how they talk in real life, too? With their families? Is this a style that's reserved just for suspects and potential suspects?

"Okay, all done," she says. "Get dressed and I will meet you outside."

Sandra finally shows up. I don't have my phone and there are no clocks in this place, probably on purpose. I have no idea how much time has passed since I made that call, but it feels like a decade.

Detective Pierce meets me right outside the bathroom and says, "Your attorney is here. Though I don't see why you need one."

"You guys never do," Sandra says, handing her a card. "If you have any further questions for my client, don't hesitate to call me."

Detective Pierce takes her card, reading her name, "Okay, then, Sandra Pullman."

"It has been a pleasure, Detective Charlotte Pierce," Sandra says without missing a beat.

I follow Sandra out of the interrogation room with the weight of the world lifting off my shoulders. For now.

6

ERIN

We have been together for so long that we no longer wonder if we are happy. We know that we are. In the beginning, I used to constantly compare our relationship, our happiness to that of our friends. Were we as happy as they were? Did we have as much fun together?

When we were first together and for a few years into our marriage, Derek and I accumulated trips.

Miami, Paris, Rome, Vegas.

Puerto Rico, Alaska, and Nashville.

Each one of these trips was carefully photographed and memorialized, by me, on social media.

There we were sipping an exotic sequin flower cocktail at the Chandelier Bar at the Cosmopolitan Hotel in Vegas.

There we were in East Sussex looking at Virginia Woolf's grave. I read her in college when I was supposed to be studying for the Law School Admission Test. I still remember how her work made me feel. As if someone finally understood me. It didn't matter that she was English and dead. All that mattered was that someone once existed who really felt like I felt.

As much as I love Derek, and I know that he loves me back, I'm not sure if he really understands me. Derek is a much more straightforward person than I am.

Things are either right or wrong.

Everything is black or white.

He doesn't get lost in the gray areas the way I do. But that's what makes our relationship interesting, right?

Who would want to be with someone who is exactly like they are?

Wouldn't that be boring?

I love wine while Derek prefers beer. He can't stand sweets and I can't live without chocolate.

He loves to argue while I hate confrontation.

Despite our differences, there is one thing that we both love to do, travel. Derek enjoys new places and new restaurants and new views. I crave it for how it makes me feel, free as a bird without a worry in the world.

Looking through my phone on this gloomy morning, I suddenly realize that we haven't gone anywhere in a long time. My phone is filled with selfies taken in cars, in front of mirrors in various restaurants, and at a few dinner parties.

Some of these photos have ended up online, but the majority remain locked in my iCloud as a reminder of how little I've done this year.

No, this has to change.

I look for flights. It's not going to be cheap, but I don't care. It's not like I'm going to fly first class.

Tomorrow is our wedding anniversary and Derek left early this morning on a flight to Philadelphia.

It didn't occur to either of us for me to come along, but why not? It's not like I can't take time off from my busy schedule (busy, being the operative word) to spend the weekend with my husband in the city where we fell in love.

Before I think of a reason to change my mind, I book a flight that goes through Chicago for $729.

It takes off in five hours, not leaving me much time to pack and get to the airport two hours ahead of boarding. When I get the confirmation email, I feel a jolt in my stomach. For a moment, I'm tempted to text Derek with the news.

But I decide to wait.

A surprise will be so much more fun! I've never done anything like this and I can't wait to see the look on his face when I knock on his hotel room's door.

My heart skips a beat in anticipation.

A FEW MONTHS AGO, I became addicted to minimalism. I watched hours of online videos about how to minimize your possessions, and accumulated various books on the subject.

But somehow despite all of this activity, nothing about my house became any less filled with clutter than it was before.

The kitchen cupboards were still packed with way too many dishes and cooking utensils and my bathroom cabinets were still overflowing with makeup samples and products, which I thought that I might use later.

The only thing that did get somewhat sorted was the underwear drawer which, unfortunately, required the purchasing of a drawer organizer.

I'm only taking a carry-on, I say to myself, so pack lightly.

I place the small suitcase on my bed and walk into the closet. My mind starts to race as I try to think of everything that I might need this weekend.

One pair of boots and one pair of pumps for when we go out to a nice restaurant. A black dress, but which one?

Lingerie. Definitely need to bring some lingerie.

Luckily, I'm not big on fancy undergarments and only own one see-through number with spaghetti straps and a flattering cut.

After laying out all the things I might need on the bed, I can barely see the comforter underneath.

No, this isn't good.

Either I can spend another forty-five minutes organizing and thinking about my outfit choices in even greater detail or I can just bring a bigger suitcase.

Quickly, I opt for the latter. I change into a comfortable long sleeve shirt and yoga pants. Is there more appropriate attire for a white woman in her thirties to wear on a plane? I think not.

Twenty minutes later, I'm driving to the airport with an audiobook about the opioid crisis blaring through the speakers. This isn't the typical thing that I usually listen to, but it caught my attention one day when I was searching for a new book.

Given how my life has been going recently, I have a little bit too much time for reading. But that can't be a bad thing, right?

I mean, I know that I should be doing a bit more physical exercise, maybe finally taking my leggings to an actual yoga class rather than just to the couch. But nothing puts me at ease like curling up with a book and a cup of tea and pretending that I'm someone else with someone else's problems.

All the shuffling around at the airport doesn't take nearly as long as I thought it would and I find myself with more than forty minutes to spare.

It's early afternoon and I silently debate with myself if it's late enough to have wine or whether I should just settle for a cup of Starbucks.

Eventually, I split the difference. I order a latte to have now and plan to get a glass of wine on the plane.

When they start seating my row, I help a woman with her suitcase, which looks like it's a few inches too big for the overhead bin.

"Thank you so much, darling," she says after we both take our seats. "There is never enough room in these things, is there? It's either that or I have gained more than just a few pounds since the last time I flew."

I scrunch my shoulders toward my chest as I try to figure out what things I want to have out with me during the flight and what things are just too ambitious to take on during the next few hours.

The journal, which I have been meaning to start writing in, stays put. Instead, I pull out my phone and open the series that I've been devouring over the last few days. It's something of a combination of a romance and a thriller with a big dose of those delicious sexy scenes that I never knew I would like.

Instead of just reading about a murder and who done it, the story is also driven by the evolving relationship between the two main characters, who narrate alternating chapters from their perspectives. They endure a lot, both as individuals and as a couple, and with all the twists and turns, the writer makes the books impossible to put down.

"So, what's taking you to Philadelphia?" the woman asks as soon as I insert my earphones. She's not the type to take a hint.

"I'm going to surprise my husband," I say. "It's our anniversary."

"Oh, yeah? Congratulations!" she says, raising her eyebrows with exuberance.

The large shoulder pads and the colorful pastels on her pantsuit are the perfect complement to her voluminous hair, which seems to move along with her facial expressions.

The entire look went out of style a long time ago, and it reminds me of the way women dressed in 1980's movies about climbing the corporate ladder.

"Is he there on business?" she asks in a charming drawl, which solidifies her in my mind as a long-lost cast member from the Georgia-set sitcom, *Designing Women.*

I nod and before she gets the chance to ask what kind of business, I add, "He's a lawyer."

"My husband's an attorney, too."

Lawyer vs. attorney. These two titles are virtually indistinguishable except that regular people outside of the profession prefer to call us lawyers while attorneys and their spouses prefer to use the fancier term. As a lawyer who no longer practices, a lapsed attorney, I find myself torn between the right description for me.

She introduces herself as Sally and asks me more questions about Derek's practice and what took him to the East Coast.

"He has a big case against a trucking company and he has to do a deposition there," I explain.

This is only partially true, but I'm not about to go into all the details with a total stranger.

Derek practices criminal law and represents a large number of unsavory people around the Southwest. Last year, however, a guy who was hit by an eighteen-wheeler on the highway reached out to his firm to represent him in a case against the company.

Derek had previously helped him out on a simple assault case. He typically doesn't do this kind of thing, but if it pays out, there will be a big settlement at the end.

His law firm couldn't just let this case go to someone else. He's working with another attorney, who specializes in personal injury law, and they are in Philly together getting a deposition from a witness.

"I met my husband there," I say after a few moments of silence. "At the University of Pennsylvania."

"Oh, wow, that's great. So, this is a bit of a homecoming then, huh?"

I nod and smile.

Philly holds a special place in my heart. Not only is it the place where Derek and I met, but it's also the city of my dream school.

I'd wanted to go there ever since middle school and, unfortunately, they rejected me when I applied for their Early Decision for college.

But then, four years later, I got my acceptance letter to the U. Penn Law School. I was on my way to changing the world.

When the flight attendant comes around with the drinks, I order a glass of Pinot Grigio. As I let the delicately fragrant and mildly floral liquid with light lemon-citrus flavors run down my throat, I raise a glass to my marriage.

It's time to start the celebration. This weekend is going to be amazing. One for the record books.

7

ERIN

I arrive at The Rittenhouse in the slush of a Philadelphia winter. It had been dark for hours and the cold chills me to my very bones. The ride share car drops me off right by the hotel and I hustle inside as the doorman helps me with my bag.

Rittenhouse Square is a beautiful neighborhood that entirely surrounds a small park with benches and tall trees. It's a reprieve from the hustle of the modern city and its high skyscrapers and busy people, and it's one of my favorite areas of Philly.

It's also a favorite of Derek's as this is the place where he chose to stay. This hotel isn't far away from Center City, about a twenty minute walk, but it's a world apart.

The Square exudes old-world charm and class, and it's very unlike our cookie-cutter new construction suburb back home in Palm Valley. As I walk into the elegant, wood-varnished lobby, I wonder how we ever ended up there.

Many years ago, while we were living in the University of Pennsylvania graduate student housing, we would walk hand in hand around Rittenhouse Square and occasionally pop into this hotel for a drink or two around happy hour.

"After graduation, we will get a pre-war apartment with thick crown-molding and oversized windows along one of the tiny streets just off of the Square," he used to say.

Our charming little apartment would be steeped in history and decorated with one of a kind finds from the antique markets we would visit on weekends. But things didn't quite turn out like that.

After graduation, a firm in Palm Valley, a Southern California desert community, offered us thirty-thousand more each than any firm did in Philly and with over a combined half a million dollars in student loans looming over our heads, we couldn't say no.

So, we packed our bags and moved into a 2500 square foot three bedroom, two bath house with a two car garage, central air, and laundry room for a third of the cost of a historic one-bedroom apartment with a window AC and a laundromat down the street, which we had our eye on back east.

Instead of heading to the front, I go straight into the bathroom located just to the left of the lobby. I don't want the person at the front desk to let Derek know that I'm coming.

This is a surprise after all.

Luckily, he always sends me a copy of the itinerary wherever he travels and I know exactly where he is staying. Unlike the airport bathrooms, the tiny stalls in this old hotel cannot possibly accommodate me and my large suitcase so I leave it outside.

Taking off my travel clothes and putting on a fresh pair of underwear with a lacy bra to match seemed like a much better plan in the car than it does now as I scramble around, trying to figure out how exactly all these things are supposed to fit on one tiny hook.

Pressing my head to the door, I try to make sure that there is no one else in the bathroom before opening the door.

I examine myself in the mirror.

This is definitely not my usual getup.

The black lacy thong and push-up bra makes my skin look almost alabaster white and nicely accentuates my curves.

The only time I've been a size four was during my first year of practicing law when I got so sick with the flu, I lost fifteen pounds.

I don't have a trench coat on hand to complete the look, but my puffy, thigh-length coat will do a nice job.

I zip it up directly over my skin, without bothering with the lingerie that I brought, and click my boot heels together with excitement.

I've never done anything like this before and an unfamiliar thrill rushes through me.

Now that my body is ready, I focus my attention on my face.

I apply some foundation underneath my eyes to get rid of the black circles that have developed out of nowhere. I touch up my eyebrows with a fresh coat of gel.

I consider whether I want to try to put on the false lashes, which I've only successfully applied once before, but decide against it.

All other times I ended up with eyelash glue in my eyes. I don't want to risk that now. This night is too important. I settle for a new coat of mascara.

Unlike my face, which travel seemed to have sapped all life from, my shoulder-length hair looks unusually good. It has a nice amount of volume and even some enticing curls reminiscent of models in shampoo commercials.

I run my fingers through it, and then apply a coat of red lipstick. My lips are chapped and peeling from the dry air in the plane, but it's nothing that some thick gloss can't fix.

A few minutes later, I'm finally ready. My hands are clammy and I'm starting to perspire from a combination of a well-heated hotel, my zipped up winter coat, and my growing anxiety.

I check my email for Derek's room number.

As I scan his itinerary, my gaze focuses on the nightly rate. $950 per night.

Are you serious?

We are comfortable with money, but $950 a night is silk pajamas, turn down service, and first class travel to a private villa in the Florida Keys kind of comfort with money.

Thank God, the law firm is paying for it and then billing it to the client.

I ride the elevator to the eighth floor, clenching my fists so hard that my knuckles turn white.

The last time I was this nervous and excited to see my husband was on our wedding day.

I can't wait to see the beautiful smile on his face.

I take a deep breath before I knock on the door.

My heart skips a beat.

A moment later, a woman with wet hair dressed in nothing but a towel opens the door.

8

ERIN

Sandra shows up immaculately dressed with her hair pinned in a French twist. Her makeup is as flawless as her wardrobe. Her clothes are expensive and well-tailored. Next to her, I look like a slob on most days let alone after a night at a police station.

One drop of cold sweat runs down my spine. What if Sandra thinks I did it? I have to explain. I have to make sure that she doesn't think I could ever do something like that. When I open my mouth to say something, she presses her index finger to her lips.

"Be quiet," she whispers.

"What?" I ask.

"We can't talk here."

I follow her down a labyrinthian hallway. The station looks nothing like the ones they show on television.

There are no large open spaces. There is no collection of desks with overworked cops huddling around and making frantic calls.

What's actually remarkable about this place is how unremarkable it is. One of the larger rooms is divided into cubicles, which you can barely see over, reminding me of a call center.

"But I'm just trying to say—"

"Erin, please," she interrupts me. "Just wait until we get in the car."

I shut my mouth and follow her out of the double doors.

"Erin! Erin!"

I hear someone calling my name just as I'm about to get into her car. When I turn around, I see Christopher Flynn pull up. With that strong jaw, large gray eyes, and thick dark hair, it's no surprise that he used to model in college.

"What are you doing here, Christopher?" Sandra asks coolly.

"I heard about what happened. I can't believe they took you in," he says to me. Christopher is one of Derek's closest friends, and a partner at Flynn, Parker, and Reed. He and Sandra worked there before Derek and I got hired.

"Heard from whom exactly?" Sandra asks. "One of your corrupt cop friends?"

"Oh, c'mon, Sandy. Just because I have a good relationship with the police department doesn't mean anything."

"You're a defense attorney. You're not doing your job right if you have a good relationship with the police," she barks. "And my name's Sandra."

Sandra starts the engine before I close the passenger door.

"Are you okay, Erin?" he whispers. "Why didn't you call me?"

Something about him always put me at ease. I've disliked my fair share of Derek's friends, but never Christopher.

"Yes, I'm fine," I say. "I had nothing to do with this. You know that, right?"

"Of course not," he says. "If you need anything, just let me know."

Sandra pulls away from the curb and I'm forced to shut my door. I wave goodbye to him before she speeds off.

"He's not your friend, Erin," Sandra says once we are on the highway heading back to my house.

She and Christopher had some sort of falling out not long before she left the firm, but they didn't get along even before that.

Sandra is a straight shooter who is a little bit too narrow minded in her approach to the law. Flexibility is not in her repertoire and everything is either right or wrong.

There are no gray areas when it comes to her ethics.

Christopher, on the other hand, thinks that rules are there to be broken. And if not broken, then at least tested for weak spots.

"That man should be disbarred," she says, pulling onto my street.

"For what?"

"Anything. Everything. He's the kind of lawyer who gives lawyers a bad name."

I smile.

"What?"

"You really should've been a district attorney."

"Is that supposed to be a compliment?" she asks indignantly.

"Take it as you will," I say. "What I mean is that you're quite a stickler for the law so it seems to me that you would enjoy it more if you were out there putting bad guys in jail."

When Sandra pulls up to my house, she parks the car and turns toward me.

"What the hell were you doing there, Erin?" She searches my face for the truth.

"I have no idea," I say. "I really don't. You have to believe me."

I go through what happened again just as I did with Detective Pierce, Will, and the other cops before them. Nothing about my story changes because nothing is different. I tell her everything I told them. When I finish, she has the same perplexed and uncertain expression on her face.

"What?" I ask.

"Are you serious?"

I stare at her.

"Erin, you can't remember? You're going with 'I can't remember?'"

"I'm not going with 'I can't remember,' I actually can't remember."

Sandra shakes her head. "Well, that's not good enough. Not nearly good enough."

I inhale deeply. The nauseous feeling in the pit of my stomach returns.

Just because the cops let me go doesn't mean that this is over. Not by a long shot. Of course not. I know that. But still. Sandra's obvious disbelief is unsettling.

I want to tell her about Will but then I hesitate.

Sandra takes ethics very seriously and, by the way that he was acting, I doubt that Detective Pierce or anyone else watching the recording of my questioning knows anything about our history. Will pretended that we were strangers. If I were to tell her, I'm not sure if she would go along with it.

"I didn't kill them, Sandra. They…they were like *that* when I got there."

I can't bring myself to say they were *dead*. That would make all of this a little too real.

Sandra takes a deep breath and lets it out slowly. In yoga, this is how they teach you to breathe if you want to calm your heart rate down.

"You have to believe me," I say in a rush.

Stumbling over my words, my throat seizes up in the middle, producing something that's the opposite of a yoga breath.

"I do," Sandra says coldly.

"No, you don't."

"I'm going to look into this further, Erin."

There's that honesty rearing its ugly head again. She can't lie, at least not well. It's an unfortunate characteristic for a defense attorney. So, she pivots instead. I know her too well to fall for this.

"What am I going to do?" I ask, trembling. It can only partly be attributed to the chill in the air.

"Just go inside and get some rest. I'll make some calls about your car later."

Of course! I'd apparently driven it to Derek's house and the cops took it into the police impound.

I get out in front of my house with a heavy heart.

"It's going to be okay, Erin," Sandra says unconvincingly. "But make sure you don't leave the county. Not for any reason. They were very clear with me about that."

Sandra's here because she's my friend and I need her help and she's way too good a person to let me down.

But she doesn't believe me. I can feel it in the pit of my stomach.

So, what now? If I can't convince her, my best friend, that I *didn't* do this, what chances do I have of convincing total strangers of this fact?

9

ERIN

Neither of us says anything for a few moments. I stare at the woman in her thick fluffy towel, wondering if I had mistakenly knocked on the wrong door.

"You can just bring it inside." I hear someone say.

I only see his silhouette through the slit in the door, but that voice belongs to Derek.

No, it wasn't the wrong room.

I push the door open and walk past *her*.

"What are you doing?" the woman says.

"Hey!" Derek grabs a towel to cover his wet, naked body.

He never dries his hair enough when he gets out of the shower, and little droplets run down his neck, settling into his collarbone.

My head starts to spin and I feel dizzy.

"Erin!" He says my name and the blood rushes away from my head. "What are you doing here?"

"Who are you?" I ask, turning to the brunette with the smoldering eyes.

Without a speck of makeup, she is still stunning. I hate her. Not because she's beautiful but because she's *here*.

Why does she have to be here?

Why is this happening?

When she doesn't respond, I look back at Derek. He's the one to be angry with. He is the one who lied. He is the one who broke his promises to me.

"Who is she?" I ask. The loudness of my voice startles even me and we all take a step back.

"I'm…I'm Susannah," she whispers, cowering away. She looks so innocent and doe-eyed that I want to scream and tear her hair out.

Derek touches her shoulder, giving her a slight nod.

She disappears around the corner, into the bedroom.

I laugh. They didn't just get a hotel room. They got a suite!

I walk further into the room. Through the floor-to-ceiling windows, I can see the entire Rittenhouse Square.

Anger builds up within me, the likes of which I have never felt before.

Who the hell is she? What is she doing here with him?

How could he take her here, of all places?

By all accounts, at least according to what happens in movies, this is the point where I would turn around and run away.

My cheating husband would follow me and try his best to catch me before I disappeared into the dark night.

But this is real life.

I want to run away, but I can't.

My body isn't cooperating.

So, I just stand here, steaming inside of a thick winter coat which I unfortunately cannot take off because I'm dressed in nothing but a bra and panties.

Crap!!

"I'm sorry, Erin," Derek says after a few moments of silence.

"I never thought you would ever do anything like this to me," I whisper. "Other husbands do but not you. Not my Derek."

"I'm sorry," he whispers, putting his hand on my forearm.

Shivers run up my spine. Reality rushes past all the fog.

"Don't touch me," I say, shaking my head.

Just leave, I tell myself. Turn around and go.

"Why would you do that?" I ask instead. "Why would you just meet someone and sleep with her? Is one night really that important to you?"

He gives me a blank stare. And then it hits me.

Oh, no.

No, no, no!

This isn't a one-night stand at all.

"Erin, I'm so sorry. I should've told you sooner, but I could never find the right time or place," Derek says.

Blood pumps so loudly in between my ears that I can barely hear a word he is saying.

"Susannah and I…we have been seeing each other for some time."

I lean on the wall. My knees buckle and I start to slide down to the floor.

"Erin!" Derek yells, grabbing me.

These are the same strong, powerful arms that held me during our first dance and when our dog passed away.

When my coat falls open, he sees my bare skin.

My desperation is exposed; lace bra with a matching black thong accentuating the imperfections of my soft stomach.

My eyes meet Susannah's and my humiliation is complete.

My cheeks turn beet red as I struggle to pull my coat shut.

Kneeling down, Derek wraps his arms tightly around my shoulders. When our heads touch, I finally snap out of my trance.

"Get away! Get off of me!" I scream, scrambling to my feet.

THE REST of the night goes by in a blur.

I look on my phone for another hotel and everything that is at all reasonably priced is booked. So, I turn to the unreasonably priced one.

It's Derek's money after all.

And this $800 night at the Ritz-Carlton will not be covered by his firm.

While waiting for the cab to arrive, I go back to the bathroom in the lobby to change into something more appropriate and comfortable.

Armed with my uniform of a sweatshirt and leggings, tears start to flow down my face. I wipe them away, one after the other, but more continue to come.

You can do this, I say silently to myself.

You just have to get to your room and then you can cry as much as you want. But no matter what I do, I can't make them stop.

When I glance at myself in the mirror, the extra layers of mascara are now moving down my cheekbones. My tears provide them with ample lubrication on their journey.

I wash my face in the sink, cursing at the fact that I didn't bring the removal wipes.

With every last smidge of makeup gone, I'm left with small puffy eyes, pale splotchy skin, and a big red nose, swollen from all the emotions that it has just suffered through.

Perfect.

I walk back into the lobby, pulling the ridiculously heavy suitcase behind me on three wheels. The fourth one must've fallen off somewhere on the eighth floor when I ran away to the elevators.

I head straight to the front to wait for my cab, but then I hear *him* yell my name.

Just ignore it, I say to myself.

"Erin, wait! Please! Let's talk about this!" Derek shouts. But I don't even bother to turn around.

"Erin, I'm sorry." He catches up to me.

Where is this cab? I peer out into the darkness. The doorman takes a few polite steps back to give us some privacy.

"Where are you going?"

"A hotel. Where do you think? I can't get a flight out tonight."

"I don't know what to say," he says with a sigh.

"So, then why are you following me?"

He shrugs.

"I just want you to know that I'm sorry."

"You want my forgiveness? You want me to say it's okay?"

He shrugs again.

"How long have you been seeing her?"

I shouldn't have asked this.

This is the last thing I need to know.

But my needs and wants are a little disjointed at this point.

Derek doesn't respond.

"Tell me!" I hiss.

"For over a year," he says.

"A year?!" I yell. He tries to put his arm around my shoulder.

"Get off of me!" I push him away.

"Erin, please. Let's be rational about this," Derek says, furrowing his brow.

"Let's be rational? Are you kidding me?" I feel my blood starting to boil. "You tell me that you have to go to Philly for work and I come here to surprise you. To celebrate our freaking anniversary and I find you getting out of the shower with your girlfriend. And you want me to be rational?"

I don't think I've ever been this angry before.

My eyes are throbbing so much that they feel like they are about to pop out of my skull.

"Erin, please, let's talk about this," he says. "This isn't all my fault."

I narrow my eyes.

"And whose fault is it then?"

"We haven't been the same since…you know that we have been having problems."

"Are you seriously blaming me for this?"

"No, I'm not."

"I don't remember you wanting to go to therapy," I say.

"Maybe I should have."

"Yeah, maybe you should have. But what you decided to do instead is to get into a relationship with someone else. Is that your idea of fixing the marriage?"

He grabs my arm. I try to pull away, but he just holds me tighter.

"Let me go."

"Not until you calm down."

I push him away from me, finally releasing his hold. "You don't get to tell me what to do anymore!"

When he grabs my other arm, I make a fist and punch him square in the eye.

10

ERIN

When I walk out of the hotel and duck into my cab, my hand is throbbing, but I'm smiling. I'm not a particularly assertive person and I often spend nights thinking of all the things that I should've said in situations where people were rude or insulting to me.

Tonight was turning out to be one of those nights. A night of stewing in regret.

But this one punch turned everything around.

As my cab pulls away from the curb, I familiarize myself with an unfamiliar emotion; I'm proud.

At the Ritz-Carlton, I say yes to every service they offer me.

Would you like someone to help you to your room? Yes.

Would you like the turn down service? Yes. Even though I'm not entirely sure what that is.

Would you like to order breakfast for tomorrow. Yup.

Would you like to have dinner brought up to your room tonight? Of course!

After I give the guy who shows me to my room, untucks the bedspread and fluffs my pillows, a $50 tip, I plop down on the bed.

It's both soft and firm, welcoming me inside unlike any other bed I've ever lay on. But first things first, my insanely overpriced lobster omelet is going to be delivered in an hour and that gives me just the right amount of time to sink into a warm bubble bath.

As soon as the water is about halfway up the claw foot tub, I take off my robe and climb in.

I turn the lights down low and let the tears flow.

They come without much of an invitation, but this time I just let them go.

How did this happen? How could I not see this coming? Was I that obtuse or was he that good of a liar?

I run through all the possible signs of his infidelity.

Secret phone calls in the middle of the night.

Long hours at work.

Weekends away.

There weren't any phone calls or texts that I know of, but the long hours and the work away come with the territory.

He's a busy lawyer who sometimes billed over ninety hours a week.

Every month or so he had to travel for depositions. Or maybe those weren't work trips at all?

Agh, I feel so stupid! I duck my head under the water and let myself float to the surface.

Unfortunately, I resurface feeling just as angry and impotent as before.

I'm angry that I let this happen and I'm angry that he did this to us.

And I'm angry that I didn't see it coming.

We were happy once, weren't we? Or was it all an illusion? A perfect lie?

No, I am certain that we were happy for many years. Up until we started trying to have a baby.

We both wanted kids, but I wanted them more.

So, three years ago, we really started trying.

Wow, what an exciting time that was.

Nothing but copious amounts of champagne and wine and sex. Lots of sex. We thought it would be so easy.

What could go wrong? We were both young, in our early thirties. Our careers were well-established and settled and we had bought a large three-bedroom, two bath house which I was busy making into a home.

Months passed with no baby in sight. Around the eighth month mark, I made an appointment to see my gynecologist and that was when I missed my period. It turned out that I was pregnant.

We were both elated. Over the moon.

Finally, we were going to have everything we wanted. The morning sickness came.

It started in the middle of one night and didn't let up until the nineteenth week.

I was so sick, I could barely get out of bed, even with anti-nausea medication. One time, I got so dehydrated that I passed out and Derek took me to the emergency room. I was diagnosed with hyperemesis gravidarum and had to get fluids into me.

But despite all this, I stayed strong. Derek was my rock. He was always there for me, no matter how sick I got.

He even supported my decision to take a leave of absence from my job so that I could get through the pregnancy.

And then, it just happened.

I woke up in a pool of blood.

He called 911 and the ambulance took me to the ER. But it was too late. I had lost the baby.

Miscarriages are very common. They happen to a lot of couples. At least that's what I learned later. But it didn't feel normal at the time.

I felt like we were the only ones going through this. And worse yet, I felt like I was going through it all alone.

Even though Derek was there for me so much during the pregnancy, he completely checked out after I lost the baby. He buried himself in his work and avoided coming home.

I was too distraught to go back to work so I continued with my leave. After a few months, when the pain not so much subsided but was buried away somewhere deep and inaccessible, we decided to try again.

Seven weeks into that pregnancy, I lost the baby again. We stopped trying after that.

What was the point, right?

If something were to happen then it would happen. But trying and mourning each attempt was just a bit too much disappointment to deal with.

Derek buried himself in his work and I did my best to stay busy without actually going back to work. I have spent the last year and a half designing, remodeling, and decorating our house to make it into a home.

What started out as a project that I was genuinely excited about, actually ended up being something I hated.

Kind of like the law.

In high school, I was fascinated with being an attorney, devouring every legal thriller I could get my hands on. My enthusiasm sustained itself throughout college and a bit into law school, but quickly started to wane as soon I started studying for the bar. Once I passed and started to work for real, it disappeared entirely.

Unlike in a John Grisham novel, my work did not take me on exciting assignments to uncover conspiracies. I did not save innocent people from death row. What I did instead was check paperwork. I formatted briefs that other, more experienced, lawyers wrote and occasionally proofread those briefs. When the firm got a few clients with estate planning needs, I interviewed them, compiled notes on who they wanted to leave their money to, and then handed over the actual work of writing their wills to someone else.

My first pregnancy was just the excuse that I needed to quit. I looked forward to starting a new life as a stay at home mother.

But now?

What did I have now?

No child, no husband, no family of my own. Just a well-decorated house that I dreaded going back to.

11

ERIN

After I get home, hours quickly turn into days and weeks. Time just flows over me without being accounted for in any which way.

I can't remember what day of the week it is or whether I even should.

I order takeout night after night and the only thing that keeps me on any sort of schedule is the garbage pickup, which comes every Wednesday at six a.m.

This morning, when I hear the truck stop by my neighbors' house, I run out to the curb, pulling the bin behind me and barely making it there in time. I didn't have time to collect any trash from inside the house because I woke up too late, but at least they take what's in the bin already.

When I get back inside, I make myself a cup of tea and descend onto the couch feeling an immense sense of accomplishment. Bingeing on a marathon of my latest

Netflix addiction, I only fell asleep an hour before the garbage truck came, so I close my eyes and drift off.

"Erin! Erin!"

The voice gets louder and louder and my body starts to shake.

Reluctantly, I focus on the fuzzy figure standing before me. Dark thick hair.

Flawless cocoa skin. Bright red lipstick.

The perfectly tailored suit and razor-sharp stilettos.

"Erin, it's almost three in the *afternoon*."

"Sandra? What are you doing here?" I get up with much difficulty. My stomach muscles so atrophied from non-use that they actually hurt from one sit up.

"Oh, Erin," she says, sitting next to me. The apologetic look on her face makes me feel ashamed.

"This is why I haven't been answering your calls and texts," I say. "You didn't take that as a clue?"

Sandra shakes her head. I can't bear to look her in the eye much longer. I get up and head to the kitchen to make some coffee.

"When was the last time you went outside?" Sandra asks.

I shrug. "I was just out there, actually. It's trash day."

"You can't live like this, Erin. It has been months since you got back from Philly."

I shrug again. "Has it been that long? I've lost track. How is he, anyway?"

Sandra is an attorney and she was my closest friend at the firm. She's still one of my best friends. But just like with everything else in my life, I've been neglecting her considerably ever since I got back from Philly.

"He's having a hard time with the case he's working on now," she says as nonchalantly as possible.

I know that she's saying that to make me feel better, but it's not much of a consolation.

Just about the only thing I have been doing while hiding out at home is stalking him and Susannah online.

And they didn't waste much time in making their relationship social media official.

"I'm sure it will work out."

"Erin, you were doing so much better a few months ago."

"Well, I've had somewhat of a setback," I say. "You know why."

She shrugs and shakes her head.

"Erin, divorce is a normal part of life nowadays. More than half of all couples get divorced. I mean, look at me, I've been divorced twice. Honestly, statistically most people are going to be married like two or three times in their lifetime."

I look away. I don't want to hear about statistics.

"Erin, I'm your friend. But you've got to move on. It has been forever. I mean, Derek is…" She stops herself.

"No, go on, please," I say.

But she doesn't respond.

"Oh, c'mon, Sandra. Don't get shy now. Go on. What were you going to say? Derek is engaged? Yes, I know that. Everyone knows that."

"Erin, listen, I'm not taking his side on this, so don't think that, please. But it's over. You have to accept that. Your divorce is final. Derek and Susannah are together."

I shake my head. Tears start to flow without my consent. There's not much I can do to stop them.

"And do you really want him back, anyway? After all that he has done to you?"

"Of course not," I say, shaking my head. "I don't. And I would never take him back."

She nods.

"But still. It hurts so much. And I don't really know how to deal with all this pain."

Sandra puts her arm around me, enveloping me in love and warmth, something I haven't had in a long time.

"Can you do me a favor?" she asks after a moment. I look up at her.

"Can you come with me to pick up my kids from school?"

I CLIMB into Sandra's Mercedes SUV and look at myself in the mirror. I'm not a pretty sight. The big bags under my eyes make my cheeks look even more sallow. My pale, parched skin has a lackluster quality to it, reminiscent of the recently deceased. I was never really a happy-go-lucky kind of person, but now I look completely beaten down and forgotten.

On the way, Sandra stops by Starbucks. As we wait in the drive-thru line, I dig through her makeup bag for something to make me look less ghoulish when we pick up her twins.

"How are the girls?" I ask, tracing a thick line of charcoal eyeliner around my top lid.

"Eh, middle school, you know? Not the best time to be a girl."

"Is there a good time to be a girl?" I joke.

"Things were easier when they were in elementary school. Now, there's all this drama. One week they're friends with some girls, another week they aren't. I can barely keep up. Plus, trying to get them to limit their social media is practically impossible."

"I don't know how you do it."

"It would be much easier if Ross were a little more involved. But I guess I should be happy that he's at least current on his child support and takes them over to his house every other weekend."

Ross is Sandra's first ex-husband. They must've been quite the power couple back in the day, a surgeon and an attorney. But they got divorced when the twins were two, setting Sandra's law career back a few years.

"You two have such a good relationship," I say when they hand us our order. "How is that?"

She shrugs. "We got married way too young. And the pressure of twins and two careers, it just all got to be too much. And it wouldn't be fair to say that everything that happened between us is his fault. Though, I'd never admit it to him."

She's joking, but only partly.

The truth is they do have a good relationship. She's always invited to his house for special events and even holidays and his second wife actually seems to enjoy her company.

"It's important for me that my girls have him and their half-brothers in their life. And in order to achieve that, we all have to make nice."

Easier said than done.

Up until recently, I used to look around and see all of these couples at each other's throats and wonder how could they become these hateful, resentful versions of themselves.

I mean, how could they let something like a breakup change them so much? How could they suddenly hate this person who meant everything in the world to them?

How could they put their kids in the middle of all that crap?

But then I went through my own divorce. Now, I find people like Sandra and Ross baffling. Some sort of fiction. My own grief and anger has swallowed me so completely that it left nothing of the person that I used to be.

"You are a much stronger woman than I am," I say.

"No, I'm not. I just had to be. I had those two little girls depending on me and I had to move on."

Tears start to flow down my face.

"Oh my God, Erin. I'm so, so sorry. I didn't mean it like that."

"No, don't worry about it," I mumble, unable to stop the waterworks. "I'm just feeling particularly sensitive today."

We pull up to the school and get in line behind a sea of SUVs. As the kids start to pile out of the front, the cars leave one by one but the whole process still proceeds at a snail's pace.

"How do people do this every day?" I ask.

"I have no idea." Sandra shrugs.

She works from home one day a week, which gives her just enough of a taste of this craziness. The rest of the days, the kids take the bus.

When the girls climb in, the mood of the entire car is quickly elevated.

They laugh and tell me about their friends and Hazel's new boyfriend. The boyfriend seems to be a surprise to Sandra, who just raises her eyebrows and rolls her eyes at me.

Sandra invites me to dinner and we decide to go to the Cheesecake Factory.

I'm a little bit embarrassed to still be dressed basically in sweats, yoga pants and a hoodie, but with the girls in the car, I don't seem as underdressed.

We spend the evening laughing, talking about school and guys and their celebrity crushes, whose names I secretly Google under the table since I don't recognize them.

By the time the dessert arrives, I finally remember what life was like before I had this dark cloud of sadness descend upon me.

I used to know how to have fun. Real fun.

Perhaps, there's hope then.

12

CHARLOTTE

Not sure exactly what happened with Torch or why he was acting so odd. When I brought in Erin Lowry, he was supposed to sweep in and fix the situation. Get her to say something more than she really wanted. And yet he didn't. He's a good detective, but we all have our issues, our problems. He took off soon after and my shift was over as well. One of the best things about being a detective is you get to work bankers' office hours, unless there's a case to investigate at night, for which there's plenty of overtime.

We let Erin go for now, mostly because we don't have much to hold her on until more of the forensics come back. Her attorney's there and she has a good reputation. Not the sleazy defense attorney kind. Not sure she'd be my best choice if I were accused of a double murder, but I'm glad I'm not in that situation.

I get into the vehicle and head straight to the Yard House, where I have plans to meet with my father. It's been something I've been dreading for two weeks now, but I was unable to put it off much longer without him getting suspicious.

As I see him sitting in the booth with his head buried in a textbook, I put on my best smile, straighten my clothes, and act friendly.

My father is the Associate Deputy Director of the FBI who worked as a special agent and a criminal profiler for years both in DC and in Southern California. He's not the kind of person who wears his emotions on his sleeve. He would rarely even crack a smile for a family photograph, not that we have many of those. I don't know my mother; she left when I was a child. Despite his ability to find people, find almost anyone who could be found, my father refused to use those special skills to help me locate her.

We have dinner twice a month, and that's the way it's always been unless he's on assignment or I have to be somewhere for work. I had canceled two times in a row, and I know that he's getting annoyed. My father is not the type of person who takes no for an answer. I inhale deeply and calm my breathing. For some reason, being in the presence of my father has always been very stressful and an uneasy kind of place to be for me.

I can sense his disapproval as soon as I sit down. My hair is tied in a loose bun with strands out of place. Something that he does not approve of. Everything has to be tucked away, put away, made perfect. When I was a little girl, I tried my best to live up to his expectations.

I remember tucking my bed in military style. All corners, perfectly square and aligned. He came in for daily inspections and either asked me to redo it while he watched or gave me one nod, which was a sign of approval, a high that lasted me the whole day.

As soon as I sit down, I start to fidget, adjusting my jacket, my hair, and then at the same time telling myself to relax, don't worry about it. We nod at each other, but then he returns his gaze to his book to finish reading the paragraph that he has his finger on. It doesn't take particularly long, but it's enough to be noticeable. It feels like he's putting me in my place, telling me that I'm not as important as whatever this is, but then again, I rarely am.

"How are you doing, Dad?" I ask. "Busy, I see?"

"Always. You got to keep your mind limber, honey."

He uses a term of endearment, even though it sounds nothing like that at all.

"If you don't, it's going to go bad like a poorly used muscle."

Is that supposed to mean something? I want to ask, but I have long since given up reading into his cryptic messages.

After a little bit of pleasantries: How are you? How's everything? You know, questions without the need for any real response, Dad announces that he's getting a lifetime achievement award.

"Wow, that's great," I say.

"Of course I expect you to be there at the dinner," he says. "It's in March."

"In DC?" I ask, hesitating.

He nods. "Where else? The FBI headquarters."

I swallow hard. I don't really like going there. I don't like being there. Everything about it feels like this undue pressure that I can never come back from.

"Family and friends are invited and you're my daughter. I'd love for you to reconnect with some of my colleagues," Dad says.

Instead of asking me to be there for him, to support him and show everyone how proud I am of him, he makes it seem like going there is some sort of favor to the FBI, which I have no interest in doing.

"You know, I still think you would've made one heck of an agent," Dad says and orders a whiskey on the rocks. I wasn't going to drink, but now I can't pass it up.

"I'll have a vodka tonic," I say. "Muddled blueberries."

The server smiles politely and asks about our appetizer order to which Dad scowls. He believes that in any decent restaurant you're supposed to have drinks prior to having anything to eat. The server of course is not aware of these arcane rules and I make a mental note to give her extra in her tip. When she walks away, I get jealous of the fact that she only has to spend a few minutes here while I'll be trapped for a full two hours.

"Well, I have a good job, Dad," I say. "I'm a detective now. Working on a big case."

"What big case can you possibly have in Palm Valley?"

"The Valley is nearly half a million people," I point out.

"Exactly. No crime, no real chances of advancement."

"Well, I'm sorry that I didn't want to work in Baltimore or Philadelphia," I snap.

"I'm not saying you have to work in a big city. I just don't know why you want to work someplace where your talents go to waste."

"I like the department, the Lieutenant. I like that we don't have to deal with all the politics of big city departments," I say. "Plus, I like the desert and when it gets too hot, I can always escape to the mountains."

"Yeah, maybe it's got that going for it. But, when you're only dealing with break-ins a little bit, maybe a carjacking and some drugs, it won't let you spread your wings, honey."

Again, a term of endearment that makes me wonder if he remembers my name.

"Let's not talk about that." I try to change the subject.

"What's wrong? You don't want to defend your position?"

"No, I don't want to argue about something we've talked about multiple times before. This is my career and I'm going to spend my time doing what I want."

"You're hiding out, girl," Dad snaps, his eyes narrowing. "Maybe you didn't want to go to the FBI because you're intimidated by how well I did there. I get it. But, there're other government agencies available. CIA would've taken you in and the NSA. You didn't have to work with me."

"I don't know what you want from me," I say. "I made my decision. I went to the LAPD and then I transferred to Mesquite County Sheriff's Department. There was an opening to work in the town of Palm Valley. I like being here. I like that there's not that much crime."

"Why even be in law enforcement then? You can just get a normal civilian job. Get paid a lot more, consult, do private security for high network individuals. There are lots of jobs out there for someone with your experience."

"Does it ever occur to you that I don't want those jobs?"

"No." He shakes his head. "I know who you are. You're full of energy and determination. You're career oriented. You have always been a star pupil with lots of achievements to hang on your wall. What changed, Charlotte? What's different now from how things were before?"

"I grew up," I say.

The drinks arrive and the conversation ends momentarily. I break off a piece of bread, tossing a piece into my mouth. A hit of dopamine rushes through my veins, but it's not enough to make this talk any better.

I stopped trying to please you. I stopped trying to make you proud of me. I stopped giving a damn.

I think these things, but I don't say them. I spent so much of my life trying to pretend and do things that I thought would make my father happy and proud. It would never be enough and it was too much already. If I tried to beat him at his own game, he got jealous. When I told him that I got my first promotion, he spent the whole dinner talking about a big case that he had just closed, testifying against a white collar criminal who had embezzled $25 million from the elderly.

When I told him that I got promoted to detective , he talked nonstop about a mobster he took down with wire taps and a six-year-old kidnapping victim, who they found alive and well, who was sold in a fake adoption. He would always try to one-up me, even if there was no reason to show me up.

He was in competition with himself above all else. And, though he wanted me to succeed, he wouldn't dare to think what it would be like if I actually beat him at his own game.

The truth is that I got tired of it. I got tired of competing with a phantom. I would never be good enough, until one day around my thirty-third birthday, I realized that that was okay. It didn't matter.

I was good enough for me and I didn't need his approval. I was a good person. I was good at my job and it didn't matter what he thought of me or why. That's the main reason I left the LAPD. I wanted a good work-life balance. I wanted to be somewhere away from any action. I wanted to do something so low-key and below his radar that he wouldn't even bother with checking on me anymore.

Throughout dinner, he talks about himself and little else. The lifetime achievement award, a new case that they're working on. He briefly mentions the double murder that is already all over the papers. And, I'm sure that he has read up on in the local bulletin. When I try to talk about it, he shuts me down, talks over me, and then pays for dinner, leaving a measly 10% tip. Like always I offer to pay my own way and to pay and to cover the tab, but he refuses to let me do it. It's a matter of pride, I guess.

When his back has turned, I throw in an extra $20 for the tip and follow him out.

"The ex-wife did it, you know that, right?" Dad says, referencing the double murder. I hate the tone of his voice. He's talking down to me, treating me like he did when I was a child.

"She was the one who called the police, but I'm not sure. There's something about her that gives me pause," I say.

"Oh, c'mon, Charlotte,, don't be so naive! Of course she did it. She found out about the pregnancy. She's had enough of the humiliation. You already have motive, you just have to find out where she was the night before and connect the dots."

13

ERIN

Two days later, I arrive at the Federal Building. Something about spending that day with Sandra and her girls infused me with energy that I had long forgotten. So, this morning, I put on one of my favorite suits from work and did something that I've been meaning to do for quite some time, change my name.

Unlike the clerks I remember from back in the day when I used to come here to file paperwork for the partners, the woman who greets me actually seems to be having a good day. I tell her what I'm here to do and hand her my divorce decree.

"So, should I give you my condolences about this or my congratulations?" she asks in a jolly voice.

I admire her vibrant clothes and plump confident body that tells the world, this is who I am and I'm not going to apologize for it.

"I guess congratulations," I say after a few moments with a shrug.

"Listen, it may not feel like it now, but it's going to be okay. You're going to be fine and you'll be a better person for it."

I look her straight in the eyes. She really believes this and suddenly I do, too.

"Thank you," I say after a moment. "I appreciate you saying that."

The woman starts to go through my paperwork. As I wait, I remember how important it was to Derek for me to take his name.

"I didn't want to change my name to his initially," I say to the clerk. "I had been a Lowry for a very long time."

Lowry was my identity. I grew up with that name and I entered law school with that name. That's the name I had on my bachelor's degree. Was I just supposed to change all that when we got married?

"But my ex kept insisting that this was the only way we would become a real family. We had to share a name."

The clerk shakes her head in disapproval.

I don't really know why it was so important to him.

Wasn't it enough that we were getting married?

That I was to be his wife? But leading up to the wedding, I caved and became a Bryson. Erin Bryson.

That's what everyone did, right? Why not me?

"So, you will be going back to your maiden name, then? Lowry?"

I stare at her. Can I be Lowry after all this time? I mean, does Erin Lowry exist anymore?

Erin Lowry was an optimist who was going to defend innocent people and change the world. Not the bitter ex-wife of a cheater with no career or a life to speak of.

"Ma'am?" the clerk asks.

"Sorry. Um, I don't know."

I stare at the form she hands me. I could've done this name change earlier, during the divorce proceedings. But something held me back. I had been Bryson for a while now and going back to Lowry just felt…strange.

"The thing is that I don't much feel like my old self anymore, you know?"

The clerk gives me a warm smile. If there wasn't plexiglass separating us, she probably would've leaned over and given me a hug.

"You're better off without him," she says with reassurance.

"*That* you are absolutely right about!" I say, filling out the form. "I need a fresh start."

I leave the courthouse with a huge smile on my face.

I don't know why I didn't do this when we got divorced; perhaps I was still holding out some torch for that asshole. What I really needed to do was cut all ties.

Once the paperwork is processed, I will no longer be carrying around the name of the man to whom I devoted my life to. He will no longer be part of my identity.

Instead, I'm going to start a new life as someone new.

This woman is going to take charge of her life.

She's not going to mope around all day thinking of everything that she has lost.

She's going to start over and live life to the fullest.

She's not going to be defined by who she is married to, but by the choices she makes for herself.

Erin Abigail Lowry is going to start life all over and this time she's going to do things right.

Filled with a sense of possibility and hope for the first time in a long time, I pick up my phone to call Sandra with the good news.

Out of everyone I know, she is the one who has been there for me through it all. She is the one who should hear about my new self first.

Suddenly, a Facebook notification pops up on my screen.

Derek updated his profile.

I click on it before I can stop myself.

He changed his picture to a *sonogram*.

14

ERIN

I stare at the profile picture in disbelief.

Is this really happening? No.

This can't be true. I click on his name and look at the latest post.

A sonogram of a baby with the caption: *We are so excited to meet you, Baby Bryson! Love, Mommy and Daddy.*

My world crashes around me as everything turns to black.

A baby?! She's pregnant? They aren't even married yet.

No, no, no.

My head starts to buzz and I feel dizzy.

I slump down onto the steps of the courthouse in disbelief.

Only a moment ago, I was moving on with life, and now that prospect is nothing but an impossible dream.

A baby. A baby. A baby.

Derek is having a baby with Susannah, the woman he cheated on me with.

Suddenly, the reality of our divorce seems so much more concrete.

Solidified.

Derek is gone.

It's almost as if his life with me never existed. He's now going to be a daddy and the mommy won't be me.

My hatred for Derek and what he has done to me starts to burn. It builds quickly like a fire on an arid hillside and fills every molecule in my body.

I hate him for cheating on me and I hate him for leaving me.

And now I hate him for having the one thing that I have always wanted, a baby.

Baby Bryson. My whole body trembles at the thought.

That was what we called our baby when we announced it. The first and the second.

And that's what we would've called our third. No, that's what I would've called *my* third. He took that away from me.

I clench my fists and watch as the knuckles turn white. Two people avoid making eye contact with me as they hurry up the stairs.

Men aren't supposed to leave their wives for their girlfriends. That never happens.

There's even that saying, *he's not going to leave his wife for you*, right? So, what the heck happened here? Why did he leave me for Susannah? What does she have that I don't?

I bury my head in my hands. I'm so pathetic. I know that and there's not a damn thing I can do about it.

I don't know how much time passes, but eventually I scramble up to my feet and manage to make it back to the car.

I climb inside and drive back home. I can barely see through the thick cloud of tears. Sandra calls me back.

It wasn't that long ago when I had called her, but it feels like the world has tilted on its axis since. Nothing is the same and there's no way I can talk to her now.

When I get home, I head straight to the kitchen and get a bottle of white wine. I pop the cork and don't even bother with a glass.

I take a swig straight out of the bottle and gulp as much as I can before coming up for air.

Checking the cabinets, I see that I'm surprisingly well-stocked. I have two bottles of vodka, three more bottles of white wine, two red, half a bottle of rum, and some chocolate liqueur that I got as a gift from Sandra when she was in Italy.

Perfect.

I'm going to drink myself into oblivion. Maybe then, this will all stop hurting so much.

A FEW HOURS LATER, I trip on my way to the kitchen and catch myself on the wall. I have finished a bottle and a half of Merlot, but now I want something stronger.

The Merlot made me feel sappy and I need more of a pick me up. I search the refrigerator for something to spark my taste buds and find a can of some low-carb alcohol in a can with a lime on the front.

As the cool tart liquid runs down the back of my throat, I close my eyes and wait for my life not to feel so crappy. A few moments later, nothing is different. I take the can to the master bedroom and lie down in bed with my phone.

Scrolling through my contact list, I stare at Derek's number. I don't know what I want to say, but I have to tell him something.

It's not fair for me to keep all of this bottled up inside.

Some of it has to land on him, right? I dial his number and wait. It goes straight to voice mail, but a little too soon. He must have seen my number and pressed the red button to ignore the call.

I curse at him out loud and toss the phone on the other side of the bed.

After taking a few more sips, I pick it back up.

I'm just going to read some news or watch something online, I say to myself. I'm not going to call him again. I'm not.

Okay, but what if I just left a message?

I call him again. Again, it goes directly to voice mail.

"Derek, I know that you are not answering my calls," I mumble. "But I just wanted to let you know that I'm calling to congratulate you… You and Susannah… On your new baby… I'm very happy for you. Call me."

After a few minutes of scrolling through Facebook, my thoughts return to him. This time I opt to text.

DID you get my voice mail?

I JUST CALLED to congratulate you. I'm happy for you. Really.

. . .

YOU AND SUSANNAH deserve all the best because you two are just such awesome people. You are kind and respectful and loving and you don't do anything to hurt anyone.

RIGHT? Right, Derek?

I'M JUST SO HAPPY for you.

YOU KNOW WHAT, on the other hand, why don't you go to hell!

MY HEAD STARTS TO THROB. My mouth is so parched that my lips crack.

When I stand up, I lose my balance.

I make my way to the bathroom using the wall as a support and stick my head under the faucet to get some water.

There are glasses in the kitchen, but that's just too far to go now.

Prior to heading back to bed, I open the medicine cabinet.

Maybe I should take something to help me sleep.

15

WILL

I narrow my eyes to make sure that they are not deceiving me.

I've had a few shots too many of Johnny Walker Blue, but she's not someone I could ever forget. Her face is etched on my soul.

"C'mon, tell the story again," a rookie trying to be my friend urges. He looks up at me with a sick desperation on his face. He wants more than anything to be my friend and refuses to take no for an answer.

"Which part?" I ask, indulging him.

My eyes drift over to *her*.

She walks over to the other end of the bar, with her shoulders slouching. Her hair falls into her face.

She doesn't make eye contact with anyone and she looks like this is the last place she wants to be.

She hasn't seen me yet.

I try to savor the moment. When she sits down at the bar, her demeanor changes immediately. Straightening her back, she paints a smile on her face.

I haven't seen her in nine years but I know that something is bothering her. Anxiety is brewing deep in the pit of her stomach.

She tosses her hair, the color of burnt umber, to one side when a cop from another department chats her up. He's married, but everyone here keeps his secrets.

It doesn't seem like she knows him, but then again I don't know anything about her.

"The part where you finally put the cuffs on that son-of-a-bitch who decapitated his wife," the rookie says, breaking my concentration.

I look up at him. Oh, yeah, that's right, he's still here, worshiping at my altar.

"Seems like you know the story pretty well," I say, bringing the shot glass to my lips and letting the last few drops run down the back of my throat.

Johnny Walker Blue is not my usual fare.

It's too expensive for my measly detective paycheck, but it was a favorite from another life and old habits die hard.

Besides, tonight I'm here to celebrate. That ass got sentenced to life in prison. He deserves way worse for what he put his wife through, but it's the best justice the State of California can offer him.

"Next round is on me," the rookie says. I could have sworn that I knew his name when we first sat down but now my mind draws nothing but blanks.

"No thanks." I shake my head. I've had enough. But the rookie insists.

When the bartender takes his credit card, I glance back at *her*.

The cop is still chatting her up, but she's barely listening. There's a glazed expression on her face. She's twirling a strand of hair around her finger. She's bored. I remember this look well.

So, what do I do now? Should I walk over? Introduce myself? Is she here to see me?

No, probably not. But what is she doing here? The last time I heard anything about her she was still living in Philadelphia, all the way across the country. But then again, I've blocked her on all social media and purposely never looked her up.

I'm too drunk to talk to ghosts.

I need to just slip out of the side door and sleep this whole night off. But my body has a mind of its own.

"Hey, there…stranger." I walk over to her. I feel like I have swagger, but I might just be meandering from side to side in a stupor.

When she looks up and sees me, her eyes widen and turn into saucers.

The cop glares at me for blocking his game.

"What…are you doing here?" she mumbles under her breath. Her cheeks get flushed as she averts her gaze.

"A better question is what are you doing here?" I demand to know.

She runs her finger around the rim of her drink and then says, "I live here now."

For some reason, her words catch me by even more of a surprise than her presence does.

"You *live* in Palm Valley?" I whisper, dumfounded.

"Hey, listen, if you're all done catching up, we were having a conversation," the guy next to her says, asserting his claim. His words don't even register.

Our eyes are locked. I don't know his name and I'm certain that she has forgotten it.

"Let's get out of here," she says, walking past me.

Outside, it's drizzling. The fog is so thick it feels like we're standing in the middle of a cloud. This is highly unusual given that this place is a desert, but not unwelcome.

The moment brings me back to the night that we broke up all of those years ago. After our fight, I wandered the empty streets in a similar fog, eventually burying my anger in a bottle of whiskey. I wasn't there to protect her from what was to come.

I take a step closer to her. Her eyes sparkle under the streetlights. Her lips part a bit. My mind has so many questions, but my body has a will of its own.

A rush of energy surges toward her. I grab the back of her head and pull her toward me.

When our faces are so close to one another we can taste each other's breath, I take a moment. It has been almost a decade, but the contours of her face haven't changed. Maybe she even got more beautiful, as if that were possible.

Now, there's a sharpness to her features. Her cheekbones are a bit higher. Her eyes a bit bigger.

Suddenly, her lips collide with mine.

I kiss her back, wrapping my arms tighter around her. A knot of electricity starts to build between my legs.

I bury my hands in her hair. She finds her way under my jacket. And under my tucked-in shirt. Finally, her fingers touch my bare flesh, sending bursts of electricity through me.

The rain intensifies. Instead of the occasional drip that feels like a kiss, thick droplets beat against our intertwined bodies.

"I live right over there," I whisper through our kiss. "Come on, let's get inside."

When she hesitates, I grab her hand and pull her toward me.

"I've missed you, Erin."

16

ERIN

I don't know what I'm doing here. I rarely go to bars. I've never been to this one. But after driving around for a while, I saw its flashing sign and it called to me.

There are plenty of women here, many much prettier than I am, especially in my current state.

I grab a seat at the end, wanting to be alone with my thoughts. No such luck. Someone starts to chat me up and I'm too polite to ignore him.

And then…

Then I see *him.*

William Torch.

What is *he* doing *here*?

Will grew up in these parts and it's the first thing I thought of when Derek and I decided to move here.

But there are almost four-hundred thousand people who live in this valley, let alone the millions who live in Southern California and I never thought I'd run into him.

I once loved him more than anyone else in the world. This is not how I want him to see me after all of these years.

If life were fair, I would have a perfect blowout, my makeup would be flawless, and I would be wearing something tight-fitting and ravishing.

Instead, here I am in all of my depressed glory, stringy hair, disheveled clothing, with a few smudges of makeup.

Yet…Will refuses to peel his eyes away from me.

The guy next to me says something, but I have long since tuned him out.

My gaze focuses on Will. He is as tall and broad-shouldered as he was before. Yet, he's leaner now. His jaw is more pronounced. His eyes are bluer. His hair is still a dark mess of thick, luxurious curls.

He comes over and we talk. The guy next to me starts to interrupt but I don't have the patience for him anymore. I need to get out of here.

"Let's get out of here," I say.

The words burst out of me. I'm already out of the door and outside before I even realize what I've said.

The crisp air feels good to inhale. It's not until I take a few big breaths that I recognize the claustrophobia that had engulfed me only a few moments before.

Will pulls me closer to him.

We kiss.

The world starts to spin.

I don't know anything about this man whose touch I have missed so much. He is no longer the kid from that other time, our other life. And yet, when his lips are on mine…we are those people again.

Young. Carefree. Full of hope.

With our whole lives in front of us.

The rain starts to fall in sheets. Will tries to pull away, but I refuse to let him go. Through our kiss, he mumbles something about getting inside.

I am certain that if we were to separate now, the moment will disappear. I don't care about the rain. I'm soaked as it is.

I want to continue kissing him forever.

He grabs my hand and pulls me down the street.

"I live right over there," he whispers through our kiss. "Come on, let's get inside."

When I hesitate, he grabs my hand and pulls me toward him.

"I've missed you, Erin."

"Where are we going?" I ask.

"To my place."

He leads me on to a thirty foot recreational vehicle. He unlocks the small door and he holds out his hand to help me aboard. The rain begins to pound against the walls just as I ascend up the steep stairs.

Warm light wraps around us, enveloping us in a protective shield. As long as we are here, nothing bad can happen. At least, that's what it feels like for a few moments.

Will tilts my head up to his, running his index finger down my neck. Goose bumps shoot up my spine. Realizing that I'm drenched, I start to unzip my jacket but he stops me and takes over. He slides the zipper all of the way down and then carefully removes it, trying to avoid getting the rest of me wet.

"You're soaked," he says, feeling my long sleeve V-neck. I shrug.

"I'm sure you are, too."

He's about to say something else, maybe offer me a change of clothing, but our eyes meet and he kisses me instead.

With my body pressed against his, I can feel the quick thumping of his heart. I wonder if he can feel mine.

Our kiss slows down in tempo. There's no need to rush now. We can savor the moment.

But then fleeting thoughts take over.

He's an heir to a fortune, so what is he doing living here? Is he working for the company like his father wanted him to? Or is he doing something else entirely?

I don't dare ask. His answers will come with questions about me. Ones I'm not prepared to answer.

Instead, I kiss Will harder.

His hands bury themselves in my hair.

Then they make their way down my back.

His lips feel soft yet firm at the same time.

In control and yet begging for more.

He pulls me down on the couch. I laugh as we nearly tumble onto the floor. The world starts to get blurry again.

His skin feels soft but his body is lean and strong.

His mouth makes its way down my neck, nibbling at my ear. His hands unclasp my bra.

As the strap snaps lightly against my skin, my body recoils. It's as if it has a mind of its own.

Suddenly, I pull away from him and sit up.

"What? What's wrong?" Will asks.

"I can't do this," I say, burying my head in my hands.

"Why?"

I shake my head, not daring to look up at him.

"Are you married?" he asks quietly.

I shake my head no.

"Are you with someone?"

I shake my head no, again.

"So, what's wrong?"

It's because of what happened all those years ago. It wasn't his fault, but looking at him now, that's all I can think about.

It's not fair but I still blame him for what happened.

"I can't do this," I say, getting off the couch. "I'm sorry. I didn't mean to lead you on."

"Erin, wait. We don't have to do anything…just stay. Please." His eyes plead.

There's the same heartbroken look on his face that I remember from years ago.

Suddenly the walls start to close in. With each passing moment, they get closer and closer. I want to explain but I have to get out of here.

I grab my jacket.

"Can I have your number?" he yells after me. "I have to see you again."

"That's not a good idea," I say, jumping out onto the street and running away from him.

17

WILL

After years of silence, Erin exploded into my life.

Then she left without giving me her number and I buried my sorrows in the bottom of a bottle.

In the morning, with a splintering headache, my life feels like a pile of ash.

I arrive at the station, down three cups of coffee without milk or sugar, and only then feel somewhat alive. Charlotte bumps into me when I am pouring my fourth.

"I'm not pulling over a million times so you can go to the bathroom," she says, shaking her head.

"It's either that or I'm a zombie all day."

"You could drink less."

"I was celebrating," I lie.

"I know. The guys said that you left with someone. I guess you just had to have a few more when you got to your place?"

"How do you know?" I ask.

"I know you like the back of my hand, Torch."

I manage a laugh.

"C'mon, we got a crime scene to get to," she says, handing me my jacket.

On the drive over, I slump in my seat. It has been raining for a few days and the clouds are hanging so low that it practically feels like you're walking through them.

Rain is a foreign experience here, in a place where there are 270 sunny days a year. But today, the sun is hidden by a thick layer of fog.

I grew up here. I spent some of my young adulthood and my twenties on the East Coast, where the rain isn't as persistent but the days are instead replaced by sticky humidity, wet snow, and gray clouds. But I have always yearned for the year-long sun and dry air of the Southwest.

"Would she be anyone special?" Charlotte asks about the woman from the bar when we stop at a red light.

I look over at my partner of more than two years and I wonder if I should tell her the truth. Detective

Charlotte Pierce and I are about the same age and this is the first time we are both single. It would be a lie to say that I didn't have a crush on her but it would be a major mark on our records if we were to get involved romantically. Even if she were interested in me like that, which I doubt.

"Yes," I say.

I don't expect her to whip her face around and narrow her eyes. She doesn't know anything about Erin Lowry, the one person who ever meant anything to me.

No one does.

No one knows what happened between us. I thought it would stay like that forever, but maybe it's time to let some of the secret out.

"She was someone I dated in college. I thought that we would be together forever, but…you know how it is," I say. I can't quite force myself to reveal the whole truth. Not quite yet.

"You thought that you would be with someone forever when you were twenty?" she asks. "You two must have really had something."

"We did."

"What is she doing here?"

"Apparently, she lives here now."

Charlotte nods, her eyes widening a bit out of curiosity.

"That's all I know. We didn't really talk last night."

"Oh, I see." She smiles and winks.

"No, it's not like that. Nothing happened."

"So, how much does she know about you?"

"I'm not sure." I shrug.

"Does she know that you're slumming it in that RV of yours?"

She's mocking me. Few people in the department know the truth about me, but Charlotte does. She rarely misses an opportunity to poke fun.

What she really means is that it's hardly a drop in the bucket for someone who is supposed to inherit the vast real estate investment fortune of the great Torch family.

If it were anyone else, I'd think that they were just jealous, but with Charlotte I know better. She knows exactly why my relationship with my family is so tense and why I want nothing to do with their money. And she knows the extent that my father has gone to trying to bring me back into the fold.

The RV is a temporary solution since I'm remodeling my house. I bought it as a foreclosure, practically unlivable, and paid for it entirely with my own money.

"Tell me about her," Charlotte presses.

There isn't much to tell, and yet the story could fill volumes. I summarize.

"We dated in college. I wanted to marry her but I never asked because no one was getting married then. I thought we would be together forever."

My words trail off. Charlotte waits for me to continue. Now, for the hard part.

"We never really argued or fought; we just got along from day one. Spent all of our time together."

"Sounds perfect."

"It was, until something happened." I hesitate. Should I tell her? I've never told anyone but I know that I can trust her.

Charlotte gives me space to think.

"I was having a hard time in Macro Economics all semester, the math was really kicking my butt. I had a test the following day and I went to this party with her. She'd had a fight with her mom on the phone and she didn't want me to leave the party early."

"Okay," she says, waiting for me to continue.

"But I wanted to get some sleep. I'd studied all day and I didn't want to forget anything. The whole fight was so stupid."

"So, you broke up?" Charlotte asks.

"No, we just had a fight. We both said mean things. Yelled at each other out on the steps of her friend's house. And then I left. On the way home, I walked past this liquor store and I just popped in. I was so angry at her. She was being so unreasonable."

This is the first time I have ever told anyone this story and saying the words out loud brings me right back to that night. The anger I felt starts to grow in the pit of my stomach. I can even taste the whiskey that I poured down my throat, an intoxicating combination of rubber, wood, fire, and dirt.

"The first time she called me that night was around midnight. She woke me up from my drunken stupor, but I didn't answer. I was angry at her for calling me so late. Our whole fight was about how I needed rest and here she was again being selfish and wanting to continue to argue."

"You were upset," Charlotte says.

I shrug and look out of the passenger side window.

A large drop of rain collides with the glass. It rolls all the way down, making a little trail and bringing other droplets along for the ride before I continue.

"She called me seven more times that night. I didn't answer any of them. When she left me messages, I didn't listen to any of them."

"I'm not sure you were wrong not to, Torch." Charlotte takes my side. The only reason she's still on my side is that she doesn't know the whole truth.

"I didn't call her back until after my test that morning, which I bombed anyway," I say.

"Well, you had a hard night."

We turn at the corner and I see the yellow barricade tape with the words *Police Line Do Not Cross*. Flashing lights are everywhere, but no sirens. Despite the rain, since it is broad daylight, a few cops are positioned around the perimeter to keep the looky-loos out of the way of the investigation.

Charlotte pulls up to the curb and turns off the engine.

"You want to know why she called me so many times that night?"

She nods. I look directly at her.

"She was in one of the bedrooms in the back of the house and a friend of ours was consoling her. He was always such a nice guy. I always liked him."

My throat closes up.

"Well, that night, he made a pass at her and when she pushed him away, he pinned her down and raped her."

Charlotte takes my hand in hers, but I pull it away.

“She called me because she needed my help. I heard her calls and I just ignored them. I didn’t even listen to her voice mails.”

“I’m so sorry,” Charlotte whispers, reaching to give me a hug.

But I just get out of the car and slam the door shut. Flashing my badge to one of the uniformed officers, I step over the tape and look at the body.

18

ERIN

As soon as I get home, I climb into my bed and fall asleep. When I wake up, the sun is high in the sky and everything that happened seems like a bad dream. But then I look down at what I'm wearing, police-issued sweats, and I know that it's not.

I strip as quickly as I can and head into the shower. Scrubbing every bit of my body to get even the faintest bit of the police station off me, but when I get out, I can still feel it all over me.

I put on my robe and head downstairs. I start to make an omelet and see the alcohol lined up on the kitchen counter. Three empty bottles of red wine stand proudly next to the toaster. There are two more bottles of white wine in the refrigerator.

I open the trashcan and toss them inside without hesitation. All the drinking hasn't helped one bit over the past two years, but especially over the last five months.

Not only that, it made me the prime suspect in a double murder. If I want to get out of this, I need a clear head.

I look at the unopened bottles sitting at the bottom of my trashcan. They are calling out to me.

What if you have company? What if you have a shitty day? What if you need to relax? I hear their whispers, but I refuse to give in.

I tell myself to stay strong and, for good measure, I pull the bag out and take it to the trashcan in the garage.

Watching the whites of the eggs start to sizzle around the yolk, my thoughts return to Will.

What was he doing there?

Why did he become a *cop*, of all things?

Back when I knew him, that was the last thing I thought he would become.

He is from a wealthy family with different real estate investments including the Palm Valley Resort and Spa. He told me that the reason he went to Pennsylvania was to get away from all that. His father allowed him to go away for school but expected him to come back and learn about the company from the bottom up.

Will Torch always vowed that he would do his own thing, but I had my doubts. Entry level positions don't pay much and money has a way of making people do things that they never thought they would.

My thoughts drift back and forth between the man I kissed and the man who interrogated me at the police station.

When I first saw him at that bar after all of those years, the attraction was immediate.

Suddenly, I was twenty again and this life that I led until now, this lie, never existed.

And in that room? Under those harsh fluorescent lights? Reality should've come crashing down around me. But for some reason, it didn't.

Maybe I'm wrong, I have been wrong about so many things, but it felt like Will was trying to protect me. The one thing that I do know for sure is that I have to see him again.

The doorbell rings once I dig into my feta cheese and spinach omelet and I pause YouTube to answer. Praying that it's not the police again, I tiptoe to the door as if them not hearing me approach would prevent them from arresting me.

"Christopher?" I gasp. "What are you doing here?"

"Mind if I come in?" he asks through the crack in the door. He rubs his shoulders to warm up and I reluctantly invite him inside.

I show him to the kitchen and ask him if he wants anything to drink.

Pouring him a cup of juice, I'm suddenly keenly aware of just how disheveled I look dressed in an old pair of pajama pants, an over-sized t-shirt, and a robe.

I frown at my reflection in the window. My damp hair is frizzing out on top of my head and my makeup-free face is covered in red splotches because the shower I took was a little too hot.

In other words, I'm the stark contrast of Christopher Flynn who is dressed in elegant leather shoes and a slim fit suit, which accentuates every inch of his muscular body in all the right places.

Christopher is the epitome of a male peacock. Not a single hair is out of place and even his hands are manicured. From what I can see, the notion of manscaping is not lost on him and he likely enjoys a day at the spa to relax and rejuvenate.

"Do you want something to eat?" I offer just out of a sense of civility. The contents of my fridge and pantry are sparse.

"No, I'm fine, thanks. I've got to get back soon."

I glance at the clock on the microwave. It's past noon. He's here on his lunch break.

I nod. Christopher is a workaholic.

He was well on his way to becoming a partner when I started at the firm and that's mainly as a result of the fact that he billed more hours than anyone else there.

Christopher also plays almost as hard as he works.

He doesn't think twice about flying off to the Bahamas or Thailand for a long weekend. He has been married and divorced twice and has had numerous girlfriends in between.

Once at a particularly boring holiday party, I asked him how he has time for everything that he does. He just shrugged and said, "I'll sleep when I'm dead."

"I'm sorry for barging in on you like this, but I just wanted to stop by and see how you are."

"I appreciate that," I say, taking a sip of my coffee.

"So…how are you?"

Now, that's a loaded question.

"I'm fine," I mumble. Christopher and I aren't exactly friends, so the only reason for him to stop by is to get some dirt on what happened with Derek and Susannah.

He shifts his weight from one foot to another. I can feel his discomfort. He's probably wondering how long he should make small talk before he can ask me what he really came here to ask me.

"Listen, Erin, I'm mainly here to offer some support," he lies.

"I know you want to know what happened."

He shrugs. "Yes, of course, I do. Derek and I have gotten close over the last few months."

I inhale deeply.

I want to shut down. I want to tell him to get the hell out, but that won't help my cause. I didn't do anything but it looks like I did.

I was the one who found them. I was the one who called the cops.

Christopher is here to find out what happened. If I turn him away, he'll make an assumption and tell everyone that I did it.

No, no matter how badly I feel right now, I need to convince him of the truth. The more people there are who believe me, the better off I'll be. Christopher Flynn is a powerful man who is also one of the founders of Derek's firm. I need him on my side.

I take a deep breath, letting it out slowly.

"Okay," I finally say and jump in. I tell him everything that happened as I remember it. From walking through their house to finding the bodies to slipping in that pool of blood.

"Wow," Christopher says, melting onto the bar stool when I'm finished. He runs his fingers through his hair and massages his temples. "That's crazy."

I shrug. "That's the truth."

"Yes, of course. I believe you," he says.

I swallow the lump in my throat. I didn't quite realize until this very moment how relieved I am by this statement.

"Really?"

He puts his arm around me. "But I don't get it. What happened *before*? Why were you there in the first place?"

I shake my head, feeling tears welling up.

"I don't know. I really don't. Maybe I had too much to drink. Maybe it was the sleeping pills. All I remember is walking through their house. That's it."

Christopher gives me a warm squeeze.

I look into his eyes for confirmation. He gives me a light nod and a comforting smile.

Christopher and I were never unfriendly and we never had a falling out like he did with Sandra, but we were never really that close either. So, the fact that he's here for me now, and he really believes me, means the world. I put my head on his shoulder and let myself go for a moment.

"The cops are looking for the murder weapon," he says.

"It's a gun," I say. "At least one of them is."

"How do you know?"

"I saw that bullet hole. Plus, they did a gun powder residue test on me. But Susannah…there was so much blood there."

"I have a friend at the police department. He'll let me know if they find anything."

Maybe Sandra is right in that defense attorneys have no business having friends in the police department, but I'm glad that he does.

"It's going to be okay, Erin. Derek was a good lawyer and good lawyers always have a lot of enemies. Once the cops start investigating his cases more, I'm sure they will stop looking at you. It will all blow over soon."

I nod.

"But in the meantime, you really have to try to remember what you were doing at their house in the first place."

19

ERIN

After Christopher leaves, I plop onto the couch and curl up with my phone. My intention is to distract myself with a mindless pop culture quiz that's supposed to tell me who I am based on the kind of TV show I like, but I end up going through social media in search of something that would explain why Derek and Susannah are dead.

I'm no longer friends with either of them on Facebook because they blocked me for ranting on their pages about them. But I do have another fake page that I had set up to essentially stalk them. Luckily, Susannah's Instagram and Derek's Twitter accounts are public.

One of the first things I see is a link to an online article in *The Palm Valley Post* under the headline *Couple Next Door Slain in Bed.*

My heart skips a beat.

I click on the link and read it carefully. The article goes

into a pretty general account of the crime scene, saying that they had been shot while they were sleeping, and mostly focuses on how wonderful Derek and Susannah were.

He spends a paragraph talking about how close Derek was to making partner at his beloved firm and how much Susannah was loved by her students. She taught dance to four and five-year-old kids and was just about to fulfill her lifelong dream of becoming a mother.

At the end, the writer mourns their death by quoting a friend of theirs named Paul Mann who states that "even though they were only married for a short time, they knew and loved each other for many years, since college."

Wait, what?

I read that line again just to make sure that I got that right.

Derek and Susannah loved each other *since college*? Who the heck is Paul Mann and why does he know more about their relationship than I do?

Derek was pretty clear that they had only been seeing each other for a year before I found out.

Was that a lie, too? But why?

I clench my fists until my knuckles turn white.

All of these lies!

Will there ever be an end? There was a time when Derek and I were happy. At least, I thought we were. But then I found out that he was already with her when I lost my last baby. He was already moving on.

With this article circulating around social media, their feeds start to fill up with condolences and pronouncements of disbelief from friends and acquaintances. Then I spot the first statement about me from an old paralegal at Flynn, Parker, and Reed.

I BET it was Derek's ex, Erin Lowry. She was really mad when he left her for Susannah and even threatened to kill them.

THAT'S NOT TRUE. I mean, yes, of course I was angry. I told them both to go to hell and die, but I never threatened to kill them. Her statement is quickly commented on by others, most of whom agree with her.

One in particular stands out.

OMG, really? Of course. She always seemed like the killing kind.

I SHAKE MY HEAD. No, no, no.

Who does she think she is? Who do all of these people think they are? They don't know the first thing about me and they're here making judgements.

I mean, yes, Derek and Susannah are dead. We're all sorry about that. But that doesn't mean that they have to go out of their way to disparage me.

Melinda Raver, a woman I don't know, but who is a friend of Susannah's, writes:

Erin couldn't have children and that's why Derek left her. When she found out, she came to their house and killed all three of them.

Even their unborn child! I'm all against cheating and infidelity as much as the next person, but Erin Lowry needs to get the death penalty for what she did. And then burn in eternal hell fire.

This message gets over hundreds of thumbs up and comments in support of it. My heart sinks into the pit of my stomach. People really think that I did this.

It's probably not going to do much, but I open a new comment window and write:

I really don't think Erin had anything to do with this. The divorce was hard on her but she couldn't kill them. She doesn't have it in her. We should really try to wait and see and give her the benefit of the doubt.

. . .

I PRESS SEND.

Feeling somewhat uplifted by the fact that I stood up for myself, even if it was on a fake account, I turn to Twitter to read about what everyone is saying about the murder.

I know that I shouldn't. I really shouldn't.

Isn't that what they always say to celebrities? If you don't like what someone says about you, just ignore it?

But that's so hard.

I can't go through the day having these people posting such trash about me. They don't know the first thing about who I am!

A few moments later, my Facebook notifications start to ding. I go back to the page and discover that my plan had backfired.

Instead of convincing people of my innocence, they have turned on me. One of them has researched my account, discovered that it was fake, and started writing that this is probably Erin posting.

The comments that follow range from 'baby killer' to 'you're going to fry!'

A big lump forms in the back of my throat and my cheeks burn with anger. Through a curtain of hot tears, I delete my comment and toss my phone to the other side of the couch.

How could I be so stupid?

Why did I post that?

Did I really think that one statement would convince all of those people of anything other than what they already *knew* in their hearts?

No, those people and their ill-informed opinions don't matter, I say to myself.

What do they know?

About me?

About my marriage?

About what I am or I am not capable of?

But still their words continue to sting like a well-placed kick to the stomach.

20

ERIN

How is it that in a world where everyone is so keen on being an individual, we all end up living in cookie-cutter homes?

I pull into Sandra's cul-de-sac in my rented car since mine is still at the police impound. Her street looks almost identical to my own. Three to four-bedroom homes, each painted approved colors of light blue and taupe.

Each one of these was custom built, and yet it's as if we had all shopped out of the same catalog. Does everyone have the same taste in housing or do we just not have a say anymore?

The questions are all rhetorical, of course. The houses are all the same because if you want to live in a new house there are only a certain number of builders who are putting up homes in the area.

In order for them to build them efficiently and for you

to be able to sell your house in a few years and buy a new one, you have to pick the features you want out of a catalog. Plus, buying old houses and refurbishing them is a big pain in the butt no matter how much reality shows try to convince you otherwise.

In most cases, you'll also end up with an inferior result for more money.

Sandra's three-bedroom, one-level house has tile floors everywhere but the bedrooms, which are carpeted, and a completely enclosed backyard with ten foot ficus trees and a view of the trampoline and the beginnings of the Pebble Tec pool.

"So, how is everything going?" I ask when I see her, nudging at the large, excavated hole in the ground.

Sandra shrugs. "They're behind schedule. I'll be happy when it's finally done."

We're both East Coasters. Sandra grew up in North Carolina and I in Pennsylvania. The first time we really connected was when we discovered that we both grew up in apartment complexes with pools and have since identified summers with being submerged in water.

Back home, it's practically unheard of for a family with a little bit of money to not splurge on a pool. Even now, as a grown up, there are few things that I crave more than lying out on the hot deck and staring at the blue water, listening to the laughter of children. The weather is pretty glorious in these parts year round, but it's never as humid and steamy as I'd like them to be. I don't even mind the heat.

"You and the girls are welcome at my place anytime," I say. "Last summer was a blast."

Despite Derek's aversion to water, I insisted on a house with a pool, which is pretty commonplace in an area where the summer temperatures hover at 110 degrees and often tip at 123 degrees Fahrenheit. But he never got into it even then. Meanwhile, I swam almost every day ten months of the year.

"Did you go with the solar heating package?" I ask, walking around the dug up ground imagining how glorious this spot will look in only a few short months.

"Of course."

"That sounds great! It should stay warm for a long time then at very little cost."

"I also decided to go with salt water."

"The modern choice," I say jokingly.

"I know, I know. Salt water is healthier and better for the environment, but how will my kids know that it's summer without that ever-present smell of chlorine, right?"

Sandra invites me inside and opens a bottle of wine. I had promised myself that I wouldn't drink anymore, but I can't resist. At least I won't have any more wine at home to keep the party going. The twins are in the living room doing their homework with their eyes glued to their iPads.

"How's everything going with them?" I ask.

She's only six years older than I am, but she had them right after graduating from college and went through the baby and toddler stage during law school. How she managed to do all that, still baffles me.

"I never thought that I would be this person, this mom to two tweens. I mean, *how* did that happen?"

I have some idea of what she means, but not really. Time passed for me, but I somehow ended up a divorced, unemployed homemaker without any kids.

"I can't even imagine," I say.

"Be careful what you wish for," she says, shaking her head. "When I was running after two toddlers, I couldn't wait to get some free time. Nowadays, they're so busy on their devices, I barely exist."

This soft, vulnerable version of Sandra Pullman rarely comes out. Most of the time, she's a no nonsense and take no prisoners type.

"They are amazing little girls and they're going to be awesome, strong women. You just have to give them some time. This is a very difficult time. I mean, do you remember yourself at their age?"

She smiles and cuts herself a slice of cheese.

"Sometimes, I want to write my mom a long apology letter for how I acted as a teenager and for how I treated her back then," she adds.

Sandra grew up in Durham and her mom worked in the cafeteria at Duke University.

I smile. "I know what you mean. I got into my own share of trouble. Sneaking out, smoking cigarettes, vandalizing people's post office boxes."

"Yeah, that's pretty accurate," Sandra agrees. "But what about all the sulking? It's the sitting around and doing nothing that really gets to me. I just want to grab and shake them until they go out and *do something*."

I laugh and pour myself another glass of wine.

"They're going to be fine, Sandra, just be there for them," I say. "Besides, I sort of think that how they are now is not really their fault."

"What do you mean?"

"They have like a million hormones surging through their bodies. Can they really be held responsible for how they're acting?"

"Hmm, I never thought of it that way before." Sandra takes a moment to consider. "My mood was all over the place when I was pregnant with them. I felt like I was going crazy, crying one moment and laughing the next. But it only lasted nine months, thank God."

"Yep, that's pretty much how I felt, too," I say.

The words come out suddenly, taking me by surprise. It's not until a few moments later that I remember that I don't have anything to show for my pregnancies.

I take a deep breath.

"I'm sorry," she says, putting her arm around me.

"No, it's fine. It was a long time ago," I say with a shrug.

"But still, it must—"

"Sandra, I'd rather not talk about it," I cut her off firmly.

My failed attempts at becoming a mother have been talked about enough. Maybe a bit too much.

Where did all of this talking get me? More in touch with my feelings? Hardly.

The pain hasn't really gone away; it just sort of migrated to another part of me. It's somewhere deeper now, where I think it's inaccessible, but then it shows its ugliness when I least expect it.

"Okay, let's change the topic," Sandra says. "I saw what you posted on Derek's Facebook page under your fake account."

21

ERIN

When Sandra says his name, my blood drops a couple of degrees in temperature and my whole body gets covered in sweat.

"I didn't know you knew about that," I say in a hushed tone.

"I didn't until this very moment."

"Crap," I whisper under my breath.

"Yeah, right, Erin. C'mon, you have to be smarter than that. Why would you do that? Why do you even have that fake account?"

"It's something I made up a while ago. He blocked my real account back when we were getting divorced."

"So, you have just been stalking them with your fake one?"

I shrug. I feel like I'm ten years old and I'm being lectured by the principal.

"No, I haven't been *stalking* them," I say defensively. "I just went on there to see what everyone was saying. And…I don't know…they were all saying these horrible things about me."

"Erin, I have to have a talk with my girls about the evils of social media every few weeks or so when they come crying to me about what someone said about them. Do I now have to have the same conversation with you?"

I shrug.

"These people are going to say what they're going to say. You're not going to change their mind by engaging with them, especially from a fake account."

"I know that. Of course, I do."

"So, why did you do it?"

I shrug again.

I don't really have a good answer and we both know that she's not really looking for one. She just wishes that I hadn't done it and I do, too.

"The police are looking for the gun," Sandra says, getting a salad from the fridge.

The statement is so nonchalant that I'm tempted to not give it much thought.

But I know Sandra too well. She's trying to keep me calm.

Her philosophy in life is that there's no reason to worry until there's a reason to worry, especially when it comes to her clients.

"I don't know what to say about that."

"You have to tell me everything, Erin."

"I *did* tell you everything," I say, taken a little aback.

Does she really think that I could do something like this? And if she does, then why is she representing me?

"I'm your friend, Erin. No matter what happened, I'm going to be there for you."

"You don't believe me, do you?" I ask, my eyes staring daggers into hers.

"Of course, I do," she says quietly. "But some things are just not adding up."

I used to look at her, pleading for her to believe me. Now, I'm demanding that she does.

"You shouldn't have been there that night, Erin."

"Don't you think I know that? You shouldn't represent me if you don't believe me, Sandra."

"It doesn't matter what I believe."

"It does to *me*," I say.

"Okay." She nods. "Okay, I believe you."

Belief isn't a decision you can make with a snap of your fingers. It has to come from somewhere deep inside. And occasionally, to believe something is to go against what reason tells you cannot be true.

"Nothing about what happened that night looks good for you, Erin," she says. Taking a deep breath, she adds, "But I trust you."

I unclench my fist and let my hand fall loosely by my side. I didn't realize how much I needed to hear that until this very moment.

Sandra calls the twins over for dinner and the conversation quickly turns to neutral topics. They don't know a thing about what I'm going through as Sandra is a big believer in shielding her kids from the darkness of this world.

I'm not entirely sure if I agree with that, but I'm not their mom. So, instead, we talk about guys they like in school. It's a nice reprieve. Unfortunately, half an hour later, the twins disappear back to the living room and behind their phones.

When we start to load the dishwasher, I ask her about Christopher.

Sandra left the firm because of him. A law firm's reputation is largely based on the clientele that the partners choose to represent.

She didn't like the type of clients that they started to take on, the ones that Christopher tended to seek out.

One of the clients that Christopher landed was the largest environmental polluter in the state. Another one was a gun manufacturer who was being sued by the families who lost their kids to a school shooter.

The placid smile on her face vanishes. She furrows her eyebrows. "He's a pompous know-it-all who thinks everyone needs to bow down to his ego."

I shrug. "He has been a lawyer for a long time."

"I'm a lawyer and I'm not like that." Sandra gets incensed. "You were a lawyer and you were never like that."

"Maybe that's why I wasn't a particularly good one," I say under my breath.

"I'm a damn good attorney and I don't treat people I work with like crap. I don't go out of my way to glorify myself and I don't take on clients I don't believe in."

"Until now," I joke.

She takes a moment before saying, "Despite my better judgement, I believe in you, Erin."

Her words wrap me in a feeling of warmth as if they are a soft cashmere sweater. I know that I didn't do this, but it's good to have a real ally. Looking into her reassuring eyes, I know that she's telling me the truth.

"But we need to find out what you were doing there. If the district attorney pursues charges, and that's what is probably going to happen, I can't go into court with an 'I don't know' defense."

I nod. I know this, of course, I know this.

"What the hell were you doing there?" she asks again, as if I am going to magically have an answer for her.

"I'm not keeping anything from you, Sandra. I really have no idea. The last thing I remember is waking up and being there."

"That's why I need you to do something for me," she says. She goes over to her purse and hands me a card. "He's a private investigator. I want you to meet with him."

22

WILL

I show up at her house half an hour before Charlotte is scheduled to arrive, on purpose. I need to have some time with Erin. We need to talk about everything.

I'm nervous. This could be a defining point in my career. The longer that I don't tell Charlotte and people at the department that we have a personal relationship, the more suspicious it's going to be. But I have this need to protect her, to make up for what I didn't do back then. Make amends, perhaps.

I look around, make sure that no one is watching me, and knock on the door.

"What are you doing here?" Erin answers, keeping the door close to her.

"Let me in, we need to talk."

The house looks unkept, like it hasn't been vacuumed for a while. Stuff is thrown all over the place. This isn't the type-A, neat woman who I remember from years ago. But then again, people change. I bet she would've never thought that I'd become a cop.

"What's going on here, Erin?"

"I don't know what you're talking about," she says. "I thought I had the meeting with Detective Pierce in like half an hour. I was planning on cleaning up still."

"I'm here to talk to you about what happened."

"Separate from your partner?" she asks.

"I'm here to help you."

She folds her arms across her chest. I follow her into the living room: wall to wall carpet, Wayfair furniture. A little bit of art on the walls. Nothing personal, more like a well-appointed hotel room.

At one point, she seemed to care. She picks up hoodies and jackets off the living room midcentury, modern couch. Puts them in the hamper.

"When I saw you in the bar," I say, "what was that?"

"I had no idea that you lived here," she says.

"That was a nice surprise, at least I thought so. And then you took off," I point out.

"I'm dealing with a lot of crap and I have been for a while. Things have been very bad with my ex-husband.

It was nice to see you, but I didn't want to stay in touch."

"Why?" I say.

"Because, you wouldn't like this new version of me. I drink too much. I watch too much TV. I'm freaking depressed. And the anti-depressants don't even work. I don't care about anything. It's dumb. It's stupid. It's all in my head and I don't know what to do about it," she says, cracking her knuckles. She looks lost, but truthful. I can tell that she's being honest.

"I don't know about all of that, Erin, but I know that what happened to Derek and Susannah is very serious. And I'm sorry."

"Yeah. I'm sorry, too. Don't you think that I am? I mean, I wanted him dead, of course. He made my whole life a lie, but not like that, and Susannah, whatever. But they didn't deserve that. And of course I never… I did not do that."

"That's what I'm trying to find out. I'm on your side, but I need you to help me."

"Help you with what? I already told you everything I know. It's true. There is no secret."

"But what were you doing there?" I ask.

She shakes her head. "I have no memory of that."

"Do you drink until you black out?"

She shrugs. "I have in the past, but not that night."

"How do you know that?"

"Because when I called the police, I was sober. I mean, I felt a little woozy and kind of strange, but I wasn't drunk. I've been drunk enough to know that I wasn't drunk."

I narrow my eyes.

“What about Detective Pierce?" Erin asks after a long pause.

"What about her?"

"You acted like we were strangers. You're not telling her that we have a history?"

"No, not yet."

"Why?"

"Because I want to help you, but I'm going to have to tell her soon." Probably shouldn't have revealed that to her. I don't want her to have leverage over me. But this is Erin. I need her to trust me in order to find out the truth.

"Did you ever make threats about Derek?" I ask.

"Yes." She shrugs. "I mean, like a while ago, when we were still married, and I was still pissed off."

"And now?"

"I thought I was getting better, then I found out that they were having a baby."

"And so you went to their house that night, to what? Talk to them? Did you just find out about the baby?"

"No, I already knew about it. You know, it doesn't sound like you're on my side, Will."

"I am, that's why I'm here, risking my career."

She looks away from me, down at the floor, and then slowly returns her gaze, apologizing with the whites of her eyes.

"Yes, of course, I know. I'm sorry."

I hear a car pull up. Walking over to the window, I pull open the blinds.

"It's her. She's early. I have to go," I whisper.

I consider sneaking out the back, but then spot my car and change my mind. I'm parked right in front of the house. I don't want to make it look like I'm evading.

Right before I open the door, Erin looks at me and says, "I won't say anything."

I don't give her a nod or shake my head no. Both are dangerous. Instead, I stay neutral, but I know that I'm going to have to lie to Charlotte as to why I'm leaving early since we were supposed to interview her at the same time.

23

ERIN

Under the fluorescent lights of the police station, Detective Charlotte Pierce looked about ten years older than she really is. When she stops by my house, I realize that we must be about the same age. I'm mildly embarrassed by the fact that I'm still walking around in a bathrobe at noon while she is dressed in a no-nonsense jacket and a rather manly dress-shirt, which does nothing to make her look even a little bit feminine. But what do I know? Maybe that's the look that she's going for.

Having had plenty of experience at working in a male-dominated office, women who work in them typically separate themselves into two categories. There are the ones who embrace their girlishness and wear only the highest stilettos and those who try to push it away by dressing in unflattering pantsuits. I've had the displeasure of trying both approaches. Unlike me, however, Detective Pierce doesn't seem to be aiming to prove anything.

After Will leaves, making the excuse that he's not feeling well, I invite her into the kitchen and offer her something to eat. But when I open the fridge, I see that the offer was a little too precipitous. The only thing that I have in there is a wedge of moldy cheese, and it's not the kind that is supposed to be covered in mold. Luckily, Detective Pierce passes. She does take a Diet Coke, which, luckily, I have a big supply of.

I offer her a seat at the dining room table and expect to be bombarded by an avalanche of questions about that night. But she surprises me once again. She starts by asking me how I ended up here. There are some people who have lived here for generations but the majority move here to escape the pressure of living on the coasts or to play golf every day of the year.

"Ah, it's a typical story. The property prices are relatively low, the schools are good, and the standard of living is high," I say. "But we also got really good job offers after graduation."

We. Why do I still use this word? He's my ex.

So, just say that. It's not like she doesn't know that Derek and I are divorced.

Or wait, are we still divorced if he's dead? Or is the proper thing to say now, 'Derek and I *were* divorced?' I shake my head, trying to derail this stream of consciousness train of thoughts.

Why do I always get so hung up on the language of things? It must have something to do with my legal education, where we were trained to analyze and dissect each and every phrase in order to elicit the meaning that we want.

"So, you got your law degree from an Ivy League school, huh?" Detective Pierce focuses on me. "Your parents must be really proud."

I shrug. I'm not really sure what my parents are. I'm not from the kind of family that praises each other.

My dad exited my life when I was young, leaving my mom to work many long overnight shifts as a nurse. Her dream had always been to retire to Florida. When I turned eighteen, she had saved enough to buy a one-bedroom condo, for cash, on the Gulf Side and she moved there.

I moved into the dorms and rarely saw her. For a while, I thought that maybe she would come and live near us when I got pregnant. But that idea didn't amount to much so she went back.

"I'm not really close to my parents. But what about you?" I say after a moment, changing the subject.

Detective Pierce nods and then shakes her head.

"Funny thing about parents, isn't it? We expect them to be these extraordinary, almost magical, people when we're kids. And then we grow up and find out that they're not so perfect after all."

I nod. I sort of know what she means, though I discovered this quite early. When your father leaves and never calls you again, it's hard not to realize that he has a few cracks in him.

"Did your parents get divorced, too?" I ask.

"I don't know my mom. She left when I was little."

I shake my head. If only parents knew the kind of damage they inflict onto their kids on a daily basis, maybe then they wouldn't have any.

"And your dad?" I ask.

"Let's talk about you," Detective Pierce says, shifting in her seat. I can sense that she's uncomfortable and regrets saying too much.

"Is it that bad?" I ask.

She shrugs.

"Do you like what you do?" I change the subject. It's nice having a bit of an upper hand, being the one asking the questions.

"Yes, very much so." She nods. "It has always been my dream to catch bad guys. I've watched too much *Law and Order: SVU* and read a few too many Nancy Drew mysteries, I guess."

"Well, that's what your parents get for teaching you to read," I joke.

"And getting me a tv."

"So, did you grow up in Palm Valley then?"

"Nope." She shakes her head. "Washington DC, suburbs, mostly. Then Los Angeles. But I moved around a lot for my dad's job."

"Is he in the military?"

"He's the Deputy Director of the FBI. Was a special agent for many years."

"Oh, wow." I let my mouth drop open.

"Yeah, it was a big deal when I decided to follow a different path. Local law enforcement isn't exactly something that my father holds as much prestige."

I shake my head, inhaling deeply. The last thing I expected when she came over this morning was to get to know her so intimately. Honestly seems to be second nature. There's no embarrassment over who she is and the decisions she has made. As someone who second-guesses herself all the time, I really appreciate Detective Pierce's frankness and unapologetic approach to life.

"I think I said too much," she says, finishing the last of her Diet Coke.

"No, it's refreshing really. People around here tend to be nice but not really frank. It's nice to hear about someone's real life for once."

"So, why don't you tell me something about yourself then."

I shrug. "There's not much to tell."

"What about you and Derek?"

"I thought we were in love and he had a girlfriend. It's a story as old as time."

"He sounds like a prince."

I laugh. "It took me awhile to get that though, you know? I kept expecting him to come back. Not that I really wanted him back."

"That's the least that he could've done," Detective Pierce says with a crooked smile.

"I know, right?" I smile back at her.

She taps her dark blue nails on the top of the table.

"But I didn't do *that*. I wouldn't," I say.

She narrows her eyes, evaluating me, analyzing me.

"I was mad at Derek. Of course, I was. I had two miscarriages. He said that he didn't blame me. He said that he never really wanted kids. And then he met Susannah and it all seemed to have changed very quickly. But I would never kill them. I could never do that. She was pregnant. What kind of monster would do something like that?"

Detective Pierce tilts her head to the side to get a crick out of her neck.

"We found a gun in a gutter, about a mile away from their house. Do you know anything about that?"

24

ERIN

They found a gun. Her words ring in my head and my throat closes up.

I cough. It takes me a moment to catch my breath. Choking, my eyes start to water.

Detective Pierce runs over to the kitchen sink and fills up a cup of water from the faucet. She presents it to me like an olive branch. When I finally catch my breath, I wipe my eyes.

"Oh my God, I don't know what just happened."

She tilts her head, and I know what she's thinking. She just told me that they found a possible murder weapon not far from my ex-husband's house and I choked up.

I take a few gulps of air and say nothing. She is testing me. And so far, I'm not doing too well.

"You found a gun?" I ask.

"We are running your gunshot residue results against it."

"Well…good. Then I'm sure that it will prove that I had nothing to do with this. I didn't touch any gun."

At least, I don't think so.

Detective Pierce tilts her head again. I don't know if she believes me, it doesn't feel like it. But there isn't much I can do to change that. I look at the clock. She has been here for an hour. That's long enough. I'm going to ask her to leave.

"Is there anything you want to tell me, Erin? Maybe this was nothing more than an accident. I can help you, Erin."

"How? By convincing me that you're my friend? Is all that stuff you told me about your father, is that some sort of fiction like what you're saying now?"

"No, not at all."

"Oh, c'mon. Please. You're here to get me to confess. Aren't you? That's your job."

"No, that's not my job, Erin. My job is to find out the truth."

"So, why don't you go and do that," I say. "I already told you that I had nothing to do with this. So, why don't you go out there and find their real murderer."

"What do you know about Maura Foley?" she asks, veering off course. She narrows her eyes again, watching me.

"What?" I ask. "Who the heck is Maura Foley?"

"That might be the first honest thing you've said to me," Detective Pierce says.

"You need to leave," I say.

I'm tired of being nice. If she's going to insult me and accuse me of things I didn't do, I don't need to take it. It's amazing how many years it took me to realize this.

"Why do you have a fake Facebook account?" she asks as I hand over her coat.

Crap.

I clench my jaw and focus my gaze on hers.

"Because I wanted to."

"You wanted to spy on Derek and his wife?"

That word— *wife*. It's like a punch to the stomach. I don't let it knock the air out of me though.

"What's the big deal?" I ask as nonchalantly as possible. "So I made a fake account? Millions of people do it all over the world."

"But they don't use it to defend themselves to his friends online."

"They were saying untrue things. If this proves anything it's that I didn't do it. I wrote those things to try to convince them that I'm not some crazy killer. Because I would never do anything like that."

A crooked smile forms at the corners of Detective Pierce's mouth.

"It's an interesting thing," she says. "Your choice of words."

"I have no idea what you mean. But I want you to leave." I open the door. A cold gust of wind flies in, forcing every pore in my body to close up before I get the chance to pull the top of my bathrobe shut.

"You said you *would* never do anything like that. But you didn't say, you never *did* anything like that."

Once she leaves, I lean against the door and melt onto the floor. She's grasping at straws. She doesn't have anything. Otherwise she would be here with an arrest warrant.

She wants my confession, but I don't have anything to confess. Or do I?

Blood that seemed to have been pooling at the bottom of my feet suddenly starts to circulate throughout my body, making me feel euphoric. However confident I try to come off in the face of the police, the thing that I know deep down is that I still can't account for what happened right before I got to the house.

No matter how much I search my memory for something, anything, resembling what could've happened, nothing comes to me. I have no idea where I was. I have no idea what I was doing wandering through their house. I have no good explanation for anything that night.

The worst part?

They found the gun and I have no idea what the gun shot residue test is going to show.

What if I pulled the trigger?

25

ERIN

My rental SUV has a distinct new car smell, which I now suspect can be solely attributed to the air freshener hidden in the glove box. I found it when I was searching for a pen to write down his address.

What kind of private investigator doesn't have the right address on his business card? What's the cost to replace it with a new address? $10 for 500 cards? So, why hasn't this Shawn Nieves guy not done it? Is he cheap or just absentminded?

All of these questions and many more rush through my mind as I drive my not-so-new rental car to the address he told me over the phone. Apparently, he just moved into the new office and hasn't had the chance to update his contact information.

I pull into a tired strip mall that has seen better days. This is an older part of Palm Valley, with old fashioned looking buildings from back in the day when people still lived downtown.

To the right, I see a small sign above what looks like an office. The sign is clearly new, but the structure itself is tattered and in bad need of a paint job. The sign above the large bay window reads, *Office of Shawn Nieves*.

There's no indication that he's a private investigator. There's also no Esq. or DDS or any other title after the name.

Do PIs even get letters behind their name? I have no idea. I've never dealt with one before.

Who the heck is this, Sandra? I say to myself as I pull into a parking spot in front of his office, shielding my eyes from the neon Pawn Shop sign next door.

"Hello?" I knock on the door and open it without waiting for an answer. A little bell announces my presence. Inside, I find a few folding chairs against the wall and a large table in the middle of the room. This seems like a place for the office assistant, but there isn't one in sight.

"Hello?" I say louder. I hear someone shuffling around in the back. A moment later, he emerges.

He's about twenty years old, handsome, and full of confidence. Shawn Nieves has dark eyes and high cheekbones and looks like the type to run five miles a day. When he extends his hand to me, he tucks his long hair behind his ears but it quickly breaks free again and falls into his eyes.

"Erin Lowry? It's a pleasure."

"Same," I say.

"Pull up a chair. Please," he says, taking a seat behind the table.

"Is this your new place?" I ask.

"Yes, I just moved in here last month."

I pull a folding chair over and it makes a loud grating sound on the floor.

I drop onto the metal chair and place my purse on my lap. "I don't really know where to start. Sandra told me to contact you."

Shawn leans back in his chair. Suddenly, I hate everything about him. I don't even have to know anything. I just hate his demeanor and his self-assuredness. Who the heck is he to feel so full of himself?

I mean, he conducts business in a crappy strip mall next to a place where people pawn their birthright in exchange for this month's rent.

I adjust myself on the metal chair, trying without much luck to get comfortable.

"I don't really know what I'm doing here. I don't really need a private investigator," I say, getting up to leave.

But Shawn doesn't make a move to stop me. Instead, he leans further back in his chair and says, "You need my help."

"Excuse me?"

He shrugs, narrowing his eyes.

"No, you're wrong. I don't need your help. Sandra told me to contact you. So I did. Whatever good it did me," I add under my breath.

I grab the handle of the door.

"The police found a gun near the Bryson's residence," he says, stopping me in my tracks.

"Yes, I know that."

"They're running the GSR test as we speak."

"Detective Pierce told me. I don't really know what you're going to tell me that I don't already know," I say, turning around to face him.

Balancing on the back two legs of his chair, Shawn says, "I know who Maura Foley is. Do you?"

I TURN on the back of my heel to face him. He doesn't move a muscle to get out of his precarious position, but instead wraps his hands around the back of his head.

"Who is she?" I whisper. Every muscle in my body tenses up as I wait for the answer.

"Why don't you have a seat so we can have a chat?"

I slip onto the metal folding chair and wait for the answer with dread. The way that Detective Pierce and Shawn Nieves both brought up her name, I just know that nothing I'm about to hear is anything good.

"Would you like something to drink? I have some coffee. Tea. Bagels?"

"Maybe later." I shake my head. "Just tell me."

"She's Derek's wife," he says after a moment.

I stare at him, dumbfounded. "What? No."

He nods, looking through some papers in a manila folder on his desk. He pulls out a marriage license and hands it to me.

Derek Anton Bryson. Birthdate: March 5, 1986.

Maura Danielle Foley. Birthdate: April 1, 1985.

Date of Marriage: June 15, 2010.

No, no, this can't be right. My ears start to buzz and my vision gets blurry. I pull the paper in for a closer look.

We got married in June 2012. I read the dates over and over. He married her two years before he married me.

I shake my head, staring at my hand and the size seven, sterling-silver ring with a dainty bowtie on the top with sparkles of cubic zirconia. It's the first piece of jewelry I'd bought since the divorce and I haven't taken it off in months.

I got this ring at a thrift store called *Second Chances*. I've always loved thrift stores and yard sales because you never know what you are going to find there. The stuff is cheap, but it wasn't just about the money. Unlike the mall and a big box store, they offer an element of surprise.

"I don't understand," I mumble. "Why didn't he ever tell me about this? When did he get divorced?"

"That's the thing, he *didn't*."

"What?"

"He and Maura never divorced."

Derek hated thrift stores. He said they smelled. But it wasn't just the musty atmosphere that bothered him. I think they smelled like poverty and Derek was terrified of being poor.

"So, what about our marriage then? We were never really married?"

"Technically, no. He never filed the paperwork."

I can barely register the words that are coming out of his mouth. Shawn sits right in front of me, but it feels like we're talking across a busy intersection.

"Derek was still married to Maura when he married you. And he was still married to Maura when you got divorced and he married Susannah."

26

ERIN

Shawn doesn't know anything else about Maura Foley except that she was Derek's first wife. He is going to find out more, he promises me, because she could very well be mixed up in all of this. Driving out of that strip mall, through the sudden rainstorm, I feel numb. I sit at the red light watching the windshield wipers sweep from one side of the glass to the other until someone behind me leans on their horn.

Maura Foley Bryson is Derek's first wife. I don't know how this is supposed to make me feel. On one hand, I'm no longer his first wife, which is kind of a relief.

On the other, Derek is even more of a liar than I had previously thought. Not only has he been cheating on me with Susannah for a year that I know of, but probably a lot more if Paul Mann from the newspaper article is to be believed, but he also made me a mistress.

Hmm, now there's something, isn't there? I have been married to a man who had a wife and I never knew about it.

How is that even possible?

Derek wasn't the type to take a lot of work trips. He never took his phone into the bathroom. He never tiptoed around the house whispering.

So, how was it that he was married all this time to Maura?

Our whole marriage?

And why?

To what end?

Even though the rain intensifies, I don't want to go home quite yet. I drive further into Palm Valley's historic downtown and pull up next to a used bookstore. I duck inside and am immediately confronted by tall stacks of books. The small space is filled to the brim and the foyer is barely a few feet wide. Someone says hello from behind the tall counter at the far end, but I can only see her gray hair. A white cat gives me more of a welcome by trotting over to me and wrapping her long bushy tail around my yoga pants.

I've been here many times. It's one of my favorite places. Unlike the large, chain bookstores with a lot of seating and fabulous coffee bars, the magical thing about this place is that I never know what kind of books I'll find. They rarely have the newest books, but they do have a healthy supply of pre-owned tattered ones.

The pages are folded and tea-stained, some words are underlined, and the first page in the book always has a pencil-written price tag. A paperback copy of Gillian Flynn's *Gone Girl* is going for $1 while a hardcover edition of Kathryn Stockett's *The Help* is going for $5. I pick up a well-worn copy of Patricia Highsmith's *Strangers on a Train* and read a few pages. I'd seen *The Talented Mr. Ripley* movie a long time ago, but I've never read it or anything else by her. Suddenly, I'm in the mood for something psychopathic.

The words go down quite nicely, like a cup of hot Earl Grey with a chocolate croissant. I read a chapter standing here in the stacks before I purchase it. The price on the first page says $1.50. I would've gladly paid $15. When I leave the store, I climb into the car and decide that I need to find out who Maura Foley really is.

As soon as I get home, I look her up on Facebook. There are nineteen Maura Foleys on there. Four are in their sixties, one lives in South Africa, two in New Zealand.

The others? I'm not sure. They are definite contenders. But I continue to scroll down, one catches my attention. She looks about my age and she lives in Desert Rocks, California, about a thirty minute drive from my house. I click on her name for a closer look.

The woman in the profile picture has shoulder-length hair, cut in a blunt bob. It's thick and shiny as if she were in a shampoo commercial. She is smiling coyly at the screen, turning only half of her face to the camera. The summer filter lightens the picture, overexposing it in parts. It makes her skin look almost alabaster white and her lips blood red. The cat-eye glasses serve as a perfect frame for her winged hazel eyes and the sparkling crystals at the edges give her face an elegant and glamorous touch.

I hate her already.

"Okay, okay," I whisper. "Who are you, Maura Foley? Who are you really?"

I look up at the cover photo. It's a close-up of a big white cat with large blue eyes jumping down from an oak. I can't deny its cuteness. Scrolling down her page, I read the first post.

I WASN'T sure what I would do to celebrate Lent this year. But then I saw the story on the news about the foster child who was murdered and decided to raise money for foster kids to get them extra clothes and school supplies and toys that their families wouldn't have the opportunity to give them.

I GO through the rest of the most recent posts. One asks for donations to an animal charity in exchange for a gift for her birthday. A few more about a literacy program that teaches adults how to read.

Her pictures consist of a lot of selfies. I don't have access to her whole profile since we're not friends, but I see the gist.

Were she not Derek's secret first wife, Maura and I might be friends. I like everything about her profile. She's concerned, selfless, and irreverent. Her selfies aren't just of her making duck faces. The majority are funny and whimsical.

The few full-bodied pictures are a surprise. She is much bigger than the slim model-like Susannah whose every muscle is toned by hours of yoga. But the confidence that Maura exudes is uncompromising. She's not going to apologize for her size and she's not going to stop living life as a result of it.

I'm about fifty pounds lighter and I feel even half as confident as she does.

Still, I continue to scroll. To search. For what?

Proof, I guess. Proof that she was married to my husband. Or I was married to hers. Now, I don't even know. Then suddenly, something occurs to me.

Is this even her? There were a number of Maura Foleys on Facebook. Maybe this isn't even the right one.

I close my eyes and think back to that folder of paperwork that Shawn had before him. Besides the names and the birthdates and the date of their marriage, there was something else there.

The address. I saw it, I just have to remember it.

I don't have a photographic memory or anything like that, but sometimes I can bring myself to an earlier moment and remember something I didn't know I could.

Palm Valley, California

Anderson Way

But what's the street name?

Something starting with 7…that's right!

7024 Anderson Way. Desert Rocks, California

Yes, of course. That's the address that was at the top of the file, next to her name.

This Maura Foley has to be her then. I look up the address online and click on the Zillow listing. It's no longer for sale. It was purchased fourteen months ago for $349,500. It's a cozy ranch style home in what the listening agent describes as a 'highly desirable neighborhood within walking distance to the park, bike path and walking trail.'

The house itself is small, three bedrooms, two baths, and an older kitchen.

I glance at the time. It's a little bit after four in the afternoon and the sun is already going down. But the evening is not in full swing yet. Without giving it any more thought, I grab the keys and my purse and jump into the car.

27

ERIN

It takes me twenty-seven minutes to get to her house. Anderson Way looks similar to many other streets in the valley. The houses are a bit older, therefore smaller and more affordable.

7024 Anderson Way has a tastefully done desert landscape and white trim around the roof. There isn't much property but the house does stand on its own lot, slightly apart from its neighbors. The garage must be somewhere out back because it's not the first thing that welcomes you. I know that I can't linger long in front without one of the neighbors calling attention to me, but luckily the house two doors down has a For Sale sign out front.

I park next to it and wait.

A few minutes quickly becomes twenty and then half an hour. I bury my face in my phone and try to look busy. I don't know what I'm doing here except that I'm waiting. I need to see her. I need to make sure that she is the Maura Foley Bryson from Facebook.

A few minutes later, just as I'm about to leave, I spot a woman walking toward me. She's dressed in a puffy jacket, jeans, a hat, and boots. Her arm is firmly wrapped around the hand of a little girl who is prancing next to her. I can't really make out their faces from this distance, but I doubt that it's her. As they get closer, the little girl wobbles as she walks, she can't be more than two. Once they reach 7024, the woman fumbles around for the keys.

I grip the steering wheel until my knuckles turn white.

No, no, no. This *can't* be her. The woman can't find the keys so she drops her bag on the ground and kneels down. I bend forward trying to get a closer look through the dirty windshield.

A loud sound sends shivers through my body.

It takes me a moment to realize that it's coming from me. I had accidentally pressed down on the horn. Shit.

Maura brings her hand to her forehead and looks at me, squinting. I shrug and raise my hands in an apology.

"Please don't come over," I whisper. "Please stay back."

It's all to no avail. She grabs her purse off the ground and walks over to my car. For a moment, I consider fleeing but that will just make this look even more suspicious.

I roll down my window and say, "I'm sorry about that."

"No problem," Maura says with a wide toothy grin. This is the problem with nice suburban neighborhoods. Everyone who lives on the street are just a little bit too helpful and involved.

"Do you need any help?" she asks in the saccharine voice of an elementary school teacher.

"Um, no. I'm just thinking of moving to the neighborhood."

"Well, it's a really nice place to live. It's a wonderful place. The neighbors are all really nice. And not everyone's nosy like me," she jokes. "Do you have any kids?"

I let out a sigh of relief.

"Um…no," I stumble over my words, taken aback by her question.

"I'm so sorry. I didn't mean to pry. I just wanted to tell you that the schools are also wonderful here. My daughter goes to daycare, but it's more like a school and we both love everything about it."

No, she can't be Derek's, can she?

"Oh, I'm sorry, how rude of me. My name's Maura," she says, extending her hand through the window.

"Maura Foley."

My turn. I swallow hard and shake her hand.

"I'm Erin…Cahill."

At least, part of that name is a lie. I should've made up the whole thing but I don't think well on my feet.

When in doubt, I always resort to the truth. Unfortunately.

The girl starts to pull on her hand to get inside.

I lean over to get a better look at her face, but she looks exactly like Maura.

"It's nice to meet you, Erin Cahill," Maura says, rolling her eyes. "I'd love to stay and chat but I've got to go. Kids, ya know? If you have any questions about this neighborhood or anything, don't hesitate to knock on my door."

I bid her goodbye and watch as she disappears inside. I should not have told her my name and I shouldn't have let her see me. I know this. But I'm also glad that I did. I'm glad that I got the chance to look into her eyes. It's the only way I could know for sure that the woman that I've just met is not a grieving widow. She was either never married to Derek or she doesn't yet know the truth.

Of course, there's another possibility.

What if this is all an act?

28

ERIN

The following morning, I try to put everything that happened at Maura's house out of my mind. All of those mistakes don't matter. At least, not today. Today, I'm going to meet Christopher for lunch and start over.

For someone who is unemployed, waking up before ten o'clock in the morning requires an alarm clock. There was a time when I got up with the rest of the working public. I got up, took a shower, and dried my hair and put on pantyhose all before seven o'clock.

Back then, I didn't start the morning with one episode of *Grey's Anatomy* on Netflix and then end up bingeing on so many in a row that the app actually asked me if I were still there.

Back then, I was a productive member of society, not someone who just shopped and drank and watched television and stalked people on social media.

"Okay, I'm going to be this person again," I say to myself in the shower as I wash my hair before noon for the first time in maybe a year.

The hot water feels odd running down my back so early in the morning. When I step out onto the bathmat, I feel sick to my stomach. Wrapping myself in a towel, I sit down on the cold toilet lid to cool off. I haven't had breakfast yet. That's all it is, I lie.

I open the window to cool off and wrap myself in a big puffy robe. I dry my hair with a hair dryer instead of just letting it air out. It buzzes when I first plug it in, probably surprised that it has been called back into service after so long. The last time I used it was in Philadelphia, on that fateful night when my unannounced arrival changed the entire course of my life.

I apply some makeup. Nothing fancy, some eyeliner, eyeshadow, mascara, and foundation. I'm not a big fan of lipstick, so that will have to wait until I pull up to the restaurant. Inside my closet, I retrieve a long forgotten gray shift dress, a pair of black tights, and my favorite pair of charcoal pumps. I tie the outfit together with a bright red scarf and long gold earrings. When I'm finally ready, I glance at myself in the mirror one last time.

Not bad. Not bad at all.

On the drive over, I try to remember the last time I felt this good about how I looked. I hate to admit it, but it was probably in Philly. You can do this, I say to myself.

Today, things are going to be different.

Today is the beginning of something new.

I pull up to an unfamiliar fusion restaurant in downtown Palm Valley and hand my keys to the valet. This place was Christopher's idea. It's about half a block from the firm, and it wasn't here when I worked there.

"You made it," Christopher says, getting up from his bar stool.

He gives me a big bear hug, leading me to a table in the corner of the room. Holding his martini with one hand, he pulls the chair out for me with another.

"Well, thank you," I say, duly impressed.

"What would you like to drink?" he asks, waving the waiter over. "I'm on my second already. So you have to catch up."

I order a Bloody Mary without even looking at the drinks menu.

As soon as the order escapes my lips, I remember the promise to myself that I won't drink anymore. But this is for company's sake, right? This isn't the same thing as finishing two bottles of wine by yourself in the middle of the night. But I know it's going to be a slippery slope.

Taking a sip of my water, I look Christopher up and down. He's dressed in his usual slim fit suit, which accentuates every hard edge. There's a twinkle in his almond eyes and his messy hair falls naturally, creating an air of mystique.

"You look wonderful, Erin," he says with a wink.

Is that just a compliment or is it something more?

"Thank you again for meeting with me," I say, glancing at the menu.

I read the descriptions of the top entree over and over again without registering it.

Christopher is a famous flirt. He was married many years ago and has had a number of girlfriends including colleagues and coworkers. He has done his fair share of flirting with me and I always took it as just a compliment and nothing more.

Over lunch, Christopher and I make small talk about the unusually rainy weather, his recent ski trip, difficult clients.

When our food arrives, I decide to just dive in.

"The thing is that I invited you here to ask you a favor."

29

ERIN

Christopher raises his eyebrows and waits for me to elaborate. I dig into my salad instead.

"I'm looking for a job."

"A job?" he asks, taking a bite of his shrimp and pasta plate.

"I'm looking to get back to work. I can't be this… unemployed person anymore."

"Well, you were never…*unemployed*."

I stare at him.

"That's a matter of semantics, isn't it?"

"Isn't everything?" he asks, his lips forming small dimples at the corners of his mouth.

"Of course. I forgot you're a lawyer."

"Shouldn't it be to you as well since you're here asking for your old *lawyer* job?"

"Seriously, though," I say in an attempt to get this conversation back on track. "As you know, I quit back then because I was pregnant and quite sick. That didn't go to plan. Actually, nothing about my marriage did. I should've gone back to work right away, but I didn't. I guess I needed the time off. But I'm ready now."

Christopher narrows his eyes. His furrowed eyebrows make a little crinkle right above his nose.

"You really want to come back?" he asks.

"Yes, of course."

"We'd love to have you. Of course."

"Really?"

"Really."

A big smile sweeps over my face. "Wow, I thought it would require a lot more wooing, honestly."

"You are a wonderful attorney, Erin. I was always sorry to see you go."

I smile at him again. Christopher always knows just the right thing to say. Now, that the hard part is out of the way, I let out a big sigh of relief. I didn't realize exactly how worried I was until this very moment. All the tension at the back of my neck seems to vanish.

I ask him more about his cases and he complains about the hours and the clients.

"You should try to take it easy," I say. "You don't want to get burned out."

"Oh, don't worry about me. I'm a work hard, play harder kind of guy."

"Oh, I know, I remember."

"Remember those Vegas trips?"

"I have no idea how you managed to squeeze them in."

I remember how after working eighty hour weeks for close to a year, he still made time to go fly to Vegas on weekends. This man didn't seem to need time off.

"I don't know how it was that you could work so much on so little sleep."

"Caffeine, lots of caffeine." He winks at me in that way that makes me think that there's a lot more to his secret than that.

As we work on our food, I ask Christopher more about the job and tell him about how much I miss being useful and how nice it will be to have somewhere to go every day.

He listens carefully and nods and makes me feel better. I've never really told anyone this before. The thing about working is that it requires momentum. Once you are on the go all the time, rushing from place to place, eating lunch on the run, it gives your life a certain pace.

It makes you feel fulfilled and content or at least it fills up enough hours in the day that you don't really notice whether you are either of those things. I lost that momentum when I got pregnant and for a while there, I was really happy to have an excuse to not work.

I have been going non-stop since college. I worked all through my breaks and then went to law school. I applied for and endured full-time internships in the summers and, after graduation, I started my position as a first-year associate. I did all those things because I thought that staying busy was the way to live life to the fullest.

But when I got pregnant and sick, I realized just how much I needed a break. It was nice to wake up at a leisurely time and spend an hour drinking tea and scrolling through news and Facebook on my phone. It was nice to spend the afternoon reading a dark thriller on my Kindle without a worry in the world.

It was fun until it wasn't. And, now that Derek is gone, I suddenly feel the need to get busy again. It's like his death is pushing me out of my lull. It's giving me momentum to start my life over again, to do what I once did best, and commit to it on a whole new level.

When dessert arrives, Christopher asks me about the case. He brings it up tactfully just like he does everything else, but he brings it up, nonetheless. I'm glad that he did. I have been wanting to talk to someone about it, someone who knew both of us, someone who could look at me and know that there was no way that I could ever be capable of doing anything like that.

I want to tell Christopher about how bad I feel. I want to tell him that what happened to Derek and Susannah is unfair. But instead something else comes out first.

"Derek was married before."

"What?"

"I wasn't his first wife. He was married to this woman, Maura Foley, before me."

Christopher sits back in his seat, shaking his head. "And he didn't tell you?"

I shake my head no.

"The private investigator told me. Only he wasn't just married before. He never got divorced. He was still married to her when we were married."

"Oh my God," Christopher says, putting his hand over his mouth. "I'm…I can't believe that."

I shrug and fill him in on the details. He was married to Maura when he married me. He was married to Maura when we got divorced and he married Susannah. He and Maura never got divorced.

Saying these words out loud, I suddenly break out in laughter. It's deep and bellowing and comes somewhere from deep within me.

"You didn't know?" I ask after I calm down a bit.

"Of course not," he says in dismay.

"Eh, I figured, I'd ask since…you never know, I guess."

"Erin, please." Christopher shakes his head.

"Derek was one of your closest friends."

"Yes, but so are you."

"I am?"

Christopher nods. "Besides, even if we weren't friends, that kind of thing…it's unforgivable, you know?"

I nod. "They were married for years before we were," I say, nodding. "I just don't get it. How did I *not* know?"

30

ERIN

The following day, I make plans to see Will. We have so much more to talk about and I haven't heard from him since that day that Detective Pierce came early. I ask if he wants to go out, but he doesn't think it's a good idea.

"Do you want to come over for dinner then?" I ask.

We're on the phone, and he seems distant and distracted.

"No, I don't think so. I need to talk to Charlotte about our situation."

"Why? You said you would help me."

"I'm getting worried, Erin. This is wrong. I don't know how involved you are and I am risking my career."

"I don't want to argue about this on the phone," I say. "You're welcome to come over or we can meet up somewhere."

He hesitates and then a few moments later agrees to stop by.

"I'm working now but I'll text when I'm about to come. Probably around two."

I look out of the window when I hang up. It would still be bright and sunny out.

Daylight.

The sun is making him feel like he's doing less of a shady thing, but doesn't it really work like that?

I go to Trader Joe's and get an assortment of frozen dinners as well as some fresh fruit and veggies, bread, almond milk, chocolate, and some other staples. When I get back and unpack, I clean up as well. I took a shower earlier and my hair has air dried. I heat up the straightener to iron out the crinkled parts and apply a bit of makeup to my cheeks and eyes.

After starting a wash of the long forgotten dirty clothes in the laundry room, I pull the cheesecake out of the fridge and let it warm up on the counter. The kettle beeps and I pour myself a cup of tea.

Maybe Will is right. Meeting up in daylight is safer.

My heart is pounding at an increasing rate and my fingertips are cold to the touch.

I'm not nervous because it's a detective who is coming to see me. I'm nervous because it's William Torch, the man who I was once madly in love with.

I pretend to be busy when he arrives and knocks on the door.

"Come in, it's open!" I yell from the other room.

Will walks in, dressed in a casual pair of slacks and a pressed short-sleeve shirt. We say hello and he gives me a chaste peck on the cheek.

"Wow, cheesecake." He smiles.

"I'm not sure how good it's going to be, but I figured we can give it a try."

"It's my favorite. Is that what you're driving now?" he asks, gesturing to the yellow Jeep Wrangler parked out front. "It suits you."

I accept the compliment with a smile. The garage is a mess of empty Amazon boxes and I have to break them all down before I have space to park back in there again.

"You guys took my car, remember? I have no idea how long you're going to keep it so I had to get the rental. It's really adding up."

"I'd recommend a monthly lease," Will says, his face suddenly getting a serious look.

"Well, I guess it's a good thing I got my job back at the law firm."

"You did?"

"Yeah, just talked to my old boss. I haven't worked there in a few years but when I asked, he said yes. Thank God!"

"We need to celebrate," Will says.

He takes a step forward and then changes his mind and takes one back. I can see how nervous he is. I feel the same way. I don't know what we're doing here but I want to be next to him.

"This job…is that the job you moved here for?"

"Yep, it's where Derek worked, too. Christopher, our boss, and Derek were really close. I thought he would be mad at me for…everything that happened, but he's really understanding."

"He sounds like a great guy," Will says quietly. But I don't believe him.

"He is."

Shivers run down my spine. I pull my hoodie close. Will places his hand on my forearm as if to calm me down. He takes a step closer.

"Thanks, I'm fine," I say, glancing up at him.

When our eyes meet, I lose myself in their deep blueness. My smile dissipates when he takes a step forward.

We are so close that I can feel his breath on my cheek.

I don't know who leans in first, but our mouths touch. His lips are soft and effervescent. He grazes my lower lip with his tongue, sending shivers down my spine. When I finally pull away, we stare into each other's eyes for a long time. But when he leans to kiss me again, I take a step back.

"Will…I'm sorry," I mumble, running my fingers along the collar of his shirt.

"What's wrong?"

"I'm not sure…"

Will tilts his head.

I change my mind. I stand up on my tiptoes and press harder into him as I lose myself in the long and delicate kiss.

Being here with him after all of these years feels like no time has passed at all. Maybe everything with Derek was just a bad dream. Maybe Will and I never broke up. Maybe I never got married.

Oh, wait, I didn't…

"I have to tell you a secret," Will says, pressing me against the kitchen counter, burying his hands in my hair.

"Tell me," I mumble back.

"I've never stopped loving you."

I look into his eyes. He flashes that crooked smile at me, making my knees weak.

I shrug. "I'm not the same girl you used to know. I'm not outgoing and confident and fun anymore."

"No, I don't think that's true." He shakes his head. "I think you just forgot who you really are. But it was just for a little bit."

"Try years," I whisper and kiss him again.

When Will's hand slides under my hoodie, my mind flashes to all of the reasons why this shouldn't happen. He's not just my ex-boyfriend but the man investigating the double murder of my ex-husband and his pregnant wife. This is inappropriate on so many levels and yet I can't stop.

If anyone were to find out about this, it would look terrible. I'm the jilted and bitter ex-wife of a cheating bastard who made everything about my life a lie. Derek was not only married before, but secretly married to someone else while we were married. He had been having an affair for much longer than I thought he was. My life has been a lie for much longer than it ever should have been. And then there's that other thing, of course. He was still married to Maura even though he was married and having a baby with Susannah. And now they are both dead and I was the one who found them.

I hate being this petty person. This stupid woman who can't seem to get over this horrible breakup. I see these women doing yoga and shopping at Whole Foods and lining up in the pickup line at school in their third-row seating SUVs. They split custody with their ex-husbands and spend their days off dating other men and starting their lives over.

Why can't I be one of those women?

Why does everything I do keep coming back to what Derek did to me?

And now, on top of everything, I am becoming the primary suspect in their murders.

Will pulls me toward the bedroom, but presses me against the wall right before we get there. He buries his hands in my hair.

I struggle to unbutton his shirt. We laugh when our heads collide as we lean down. He pushes me down onto the bed.

Cradling my face between his hands, he kisses me again and again.

LYING in Will's arms afterward, I feel alive.

Awake. Relaxed yet invigorated. It's like every molecule in my body is suddenly energized. Infused with life.

"I haven't done that in…a very long time," I say, running my fingers lazily down the middle of his chest.

"That was…great," he says, giving me a peck on my head. "I can't believe we are here again…after all of these years."

In the afterglow, we talk about anything and everything. Recent favorite movies. Music. Pop culture. I'm pretty much caught up on all the television drama since I have a lot of time off, but I'm surprised how plugged in Will is. *The Witcher. Game of Thrones. 90 Day Fiancé*. You name it, he knows what's up.

"So, when is it that you have so much time to watch TV?" I ask.

"I have work and time off work. It's not like I have a family or anything, and I'm trying to play less video games. Have to fill my hours somehow."

I laugh and snuggle up to him. It feels good to lie here in bed with my arms around him rather than an empty liquor bottle.

"So, I've been meaning to ask you something," Will says. "It's about the case."

"Yeah, sure."

"You really don't remember a thing? Like, why you were there in the first place?"

I shake my head no. "All I remember is walking to the house and then through their living room. I have no idea what I was doing there. But I'm sure I didn't kill them. I mean…I would never do that. Plus, I didn't have a gun."

"Is there any chance that you did and stashed it somewhere?"

I sit up and wrap the sheet around myself. I can't believe that he's asking me this. Does he really not believe me or is he just trying to figure something out?

For now, I'll give him the benefit of the doubt. "No, there is no chance. I don't own a gun. Besides…I'm not…who do you think I am?"

"I'm sorry, Erin, really. I didn't mean anything by that. It's just so…odd."

"I know it's odd. Don't you think I know that? But it is what it is."

I go over everything I remember from that night in detail. Extreme detail. Every last bit. I need him to believe me because I need it to be real.

It's not that it's not. It's just that I can't have people thinking that I could do something like that.

Derek and I had issues. Secrets. But to murder him and his new wife and baby? No, that's not me. I would, could, never do that. And yet…what was I doing there?

"If you didn't do it—" Will starts to say.

"Since I didn't do it," I correct him.

"Yes, of course. *Since* you didn't do it. Did you see anyone there? Was someone running away from the scene when you showed up?"

I shake my head no. "Not that I know of."

"Whoever did this, I'm sure we will find him soon," Will says, giving me a squeeze. I put my head back down on his shoulder and close my eyes.

The sound of the doorbell wakes me up. I squint, the falling sun streaming through the window. It's later in the afternoon.

The doorbell rings again. Who could that be? I wonder, throwing on my robe. A big smile settles on my face as I head downstairs and open the door.

"Detective Pierce…what are you doing here?"

31

CHARLOTTE

I pull up to Erin's house. I sit in my car for a few minutes holding the letter. No one sends letters anymore, except for maybe Christmas cards. But she did.

There was a time when I kept up with people on social media. But as Facebook fell out of fashion and others joined Instagram and Snapchat under different names, we lost touch. That was fine by me. I didn't want to keep in touch after what happened.

But here it is, an invitation to reconnect.

Due to my dad's work schedule, I went to two different high schools and a different middle school and elementary school, and I was fine with that. At least I thought so at the time. I learned how to make friends easily and how to lose them just as easily. I didn't have too many attachments, and perhaps I was worse for that. There was always a new friend to make. Then I would move and I'd lose that friend. After a while, it was hard to care much.

I opened the letter last night and put it into my bag to keep it with me, to think about it some more. I'd recognize her handwriting anywhere. It is authored by none other than Clara Foster, the secretary and later vice president of my eighth grade class.

"Dear Charlotte. I'm hosting a dinner to commemorate the 20th anniversary of our eighth grade graduation. We have all grown up, started our lives and careers and families. Everyone wants to reconnect with high school friends. High school friends are important, but it got me thinking. What about our middle school lives? They were so important to us developmentally. It was a time when we were innocent 12, 13, 14 year olds who were just as confused about the world as we were about ourselves. I'd love to meet the grown-up version of you and reminisce. I hope that you will join us. Please RSVP to 79243 Chestnut Avenue, Long Beach, California. I'd love to see what you're up to."

I stare at the letter, handwritten in her neat script. There's a little heart above the i's, and I wonder if that's something that she does now, or if it's an homage to how she used to write her name. She uses an elevated version of the big cursive letters. When she signed my yearbook she wrote, "I'll miss you no matter what. Stay in touch."

In middle school, we exchanged hundreds of letters. We wrote down our deepest, darkest dreams and popped them into each other's lockers. We gossiped about the boys we liked and celebrities we gushed over. Clara was one of my closest friends. We were a squad that nothing could separate. We didn't really rule the school, but we hung out on the sidelines, mocking the popular kids, secretly being jealous of them. I thought we'd be friends forever.

Then something happened; something that I will never forget. That's what drove me away from this place, forced me to start my life over. That's why I vow to never go back. But now I'm not so sure. Maybe it's time to reconcile with the past, to make amends.

If not now, then when? Is that what Clara's letter means?

Does she want to talk about the horrible thing that we did?

Does she want to get past it as much I do? And what about the others?

I fold the letter neatly back into the envelope that I have so haphazardly ripped in two, tucking it back safely into my cross-body bag I step out of the car.

Walking up the steps, I knock on the door loudly, trying to put everything having to do with the letter out of my mind. Erin answers and then Will appears, the last person that I expect.

How did I not see his car parked right out front? I glance back briefly recognizing it immediately.

"What are you doing here?" I ask him.

"Got here early. I have to go now. Can't stay."

"Why?"

"I'll tell you later."

He gives me a wink, that self-assured smile like everything is going to be okay. I try to give him the benefit of the doubt, but as soon as I look at Erin, I know that something's off.

Erin shifts her weight from one foot to another. She looks nervous, even more than usual. Dressed in a bathrobe, pink terry cloth, she pulls at her belt a little bit at a time in an anxious fashion while at the same time picking at her cuticles. Her hair is messed up and underneath the robe she's wearing black yoga pants. She's barefoot. The nail polish on her toenails is peeling.

I try to remember what Will's attire looked like earlier. Disheveled in any way or professional? I was so surprised to see him, but nothing comes to mind.

What were you doing here, Will? I say silently to myself. I intend to ask, but I don't want to make it seem like we didn't have this planned, like there's something off.

Something is going on that I don't know about. Did he come here early to discuss the case with her?

She offers me some coffee and I decline. She puts hot water in a kettle for tea for herself and doesn't offer me any. I beat around the bush a little bit. I want to come right out and question her about the positive gun powder residue test but bide my time.

"How's everything going with you?" I ask. "How are you holding up?"

I'm trying to make a friend, however tenuously.

"I'm fine. Still quite shaken up about Derek and Susannah, but you know, just trying to make the best of it."

"Yeah, I understand. Have you given any more thought to what could have happened that night? Any memories spring up?"

"No, not at all. I've been thinking about it and it's like it all happened to someone else. I'm just really torn up."

“Yes, of course,” I say, pretending to be understanding, comforting, because what else can I do?

When there’s a lull in the conversation, I jump right to the point.

"Why was Will here?" I ask. Her eyes flash up.

"He said that he had to stop by early,” she says.

It's important to have trust between two detectives investigating the same case. The stories we tell the suspects have to line up. They have to make sense.

Otherwise, they'll figure everything out.

"I'm here to talk to you about the GSR test result. It came back positive."

Erin's face turns ashen white and she looks shaken. She licks her lower lip, a dry patch in bad need of lip gloss, some sort of relief of any kind.

"What does that mean?" she asks after a long pause. Pulling at her robe, she leans against the counter to appease some of her nervousness.

"I just don't even understand how that could have happened."

"A positive result for GSR from SEM-EDX analysis can mean a number of things. Mainly it indicates that a person either handled a gun after it was fired or was in the vicinity of a gun when it was fired. Can you tell me why you would've tested positive for GSR?"

"I have no idea. I told you I don't remember much, but I neither handled the gun nor was in the vicinity of any gun."

"But how can you know for sure?" I ask. "I mean, you said that you don't remember."

"Yes, I did. But I'm certain about that."

"Really? How so?"

Erin tilts her head and gives me a blank stare.

You were there. You were the one who held the gun, I want to say, but not yet. If she wants to feign innocence, if she wants to pretend that she had nothing to do with this, I'll play along. Sure. Why not?

Maybe she'll admit to something that she shouldn't have.

Maybe she'll make a mistake.

She offered me coffee before and now I wish that I had taken her up on it. It would've made it harder for her to kick me out if I got out of line, asked her too many unwanted questions, and now all she has to do is say, 'please leave.' And the conversation will be over.

I have no arrest warrant. I have no way to push any of this forward, but Erin doesn't. She just keeps playing with the belt of her robe, picking at the little fluff on the edges.

I decide to release some of the pressure by asking about Will again.

"Why did he come? What did you ask? What did he ask you?" But she freezes up.

"I really can't talk about this anymore, Detective Pierce. I have an attorney now and I need to protect myself. I feel like you're trying to entrap me into some situation and make me part of something that I never was part of."

"That's not what I'm doing, Erin. I'm on your side."

"It doesn't feel like that," she says. "I'd like for you to leave."

Crap, I say silently to myself.

I hesitate to try to find another reason to stay, but I know that if she were to come out and admit something to me right here and now I would be in big trouble. Not only did she retain an attorney, but she also asked me to leave and said that she doesn't want to say another word without her presence.

No, I shouldn't push this anymore. I should go and talk to Will and find out what it is that he knows.

32

CHARLOTTE

I get in the car and drive straight to the station, where I find Will having lunch at his desk. Not wanting to make a scene and not wanting to talk about this in a hushed tone either, I ask him if he wants to grab some coffee with me.

"No, I'm good," Will says, waving his hand and turning his eyes back to his laptop.

Is he being dense on purpose? Probably, but I'm not going to let it slide.

"I really need to talk to you. You mind coming?" I ask again, my tone of voice more forceful this time.

I can feel him hesitating, but he tosses the last bit of his sandwich in his mouth, wads up the bag into a little ball, and tosses it in the trash, as if he were dunking a basketball.

We walk past the coffee stand and I lead him out to the parking lot and further away from the police station.

Please don't be involved with this, please don't be involved with this, I repeat over and over as if it's my mantra.

Will and I have formed a real friendship over this past two years that we've worked together. No romantic entanglements, which is surprising for both him and me, given our mutual tendencies to get involved in improper relationships. It's almost as if we both made a promise to ourselves that this is one relationship we're not messing up.

It would be a lie to say that I didn't have certain feelings for him at certain points, but I had kept them at bay. It was better this way. I've messed up every relationship I've ever had and gotten involved in a number of toxic ones as well with selfish men, full of lies and secrets.

I never dated anyone who was married though, which I wear as a badge of honor. I hate cheaters. They're liars to the nth degree. If they'll cheat with you, they'll cheat on you. It's one of those old sayings that I wholeheartedly endorse. I never wanted any part of that.

There's a big park with baseball fields right outside the station, a couple of ponds, picnic tables, and two playgrounds for little kids of different ages, as well as basketball courts. This is the hub of civic life here, the station being positioned right next to City Hall and the park.

"Come," I say and lead him closer to the ducks and the pond.

As soon as we get to the little bridge underneath where the turtles gather, I lean over the railing, stare out into the distance, and ask him, "What's going on with you and Erin?"

"I don't know what you're talking about—" Will starts to say.

I turn to face him. He leans over the bridge as well. A man in a yellow jacket on a bicycle rides by. I hesitate for a moment before turning my attention back to Will.

His hair's grown out. He's got a five o'clock shadow. He looks unkempt, not unusual for a detective, since the rules of conduct and appearance are a little bit more lax. But still, he doesn't look like he's slept in a day, and the bags under his eyes are pronounced.

"Why were you at her house?"

"To get a statement, I had a doctor's appointment after."

Will's had his share of heartbreak, cheating girlfriends, and a fiancée. We got together more than a couple times at the bar to lick our wounds and complain to each other about all the bad relationships that we have had. But we never crossed the line.

Not even close, not even once. I now consider him one of my best friends.

No, my *best* friend.

He is someone who has always been there to listen and challenge me in that way that good friends can.

Never, not until now, did I ever think that we would ever keep secrets from one another. And now I feel like I'm on the verge of finding out the truth about the only man that never lied to me and I kind of hate it.

"I know you, Will," I say. "I know you well, I'm your friend. I also know that this isn't you. Something is off. You don't want me going on with this investigation any further, without knowing everything."

"Look, there's nothing wrong with me being there. I had to talk to Erin. I couldn't make it at the time you and I agreed to."

"If I don't trust you as my partner, as my friend, as someone who enforces the law, that's not good, and you know that. I want to trust you, Will, and you can trust me."

"No, I can't." He shakes his head.

"Why not?"

"I can't tell you what's going on, Charlotte. It'll put your career at risk."

“So, something *is* going on. Something indecent? Illegal?"

"Improper is more like it.” He swallows hard, his Adam's apple moving up and down.

"Why won't you tell me?" I say after a long pause.

Appealing to him as a friend will probably have the best result, and I can't analyze the situation as a detective right now. There’re a million different thoughts running through my mind.

"It's hard for me to say," he says, "but I want to protect you. I don't want to make this any more difficult than it has to be."

"Neither do I," I say. "What's going on? Why is everything so convoluted?"

"Erin and I…” Will starts to say, and then shuts down again. "If I tell you this, you could lose your badge, especially if you protect me. Can you just let it go? Can you just do that?"

I hesitate.

"Whatever's going on is very serious, and you're jeopardizing the investigation,” I say after a pause. “You're protecting her; you can't do that."

"I can't," he says. "I'm not doing anything illegal. Improper, maybe, yes, but I have certain debts that I have to pay; can you please understand that?"

"I want to, I really do," I say, "but it's more complicated than that."

I GIVE UP ON WILL. He's not going to come through. He's not going to tell me the truth. But whatever is going on, it's something serious. He said that he doesn't want to incriminate me; he doesn't want to make me part of the problem. But what does that mean?

We head back to the station. I walk slightly to the side, trying to think of one last thing to say to get him to change his mind.

"Are you sleeping with her?" the words spring out of me.

We just walked over the threshold, not quite at the front desk, but no longer in private. He flashes his eyes back at me, glaring.

"What are you talking about?" he hisses.

"Is that what's going on? Is it that bad?"

When Will swallows, his Adam's apple moves up and down again.

His eyes dart from side to side. I know him well enough to know that I'm onto something.

The hallway is empty for now, but it's anything but a private space.

"Tell me what happened," I say a little too loudly, leaving it up to him to take precautions against someone overhearing our conversation.

I'm trying to add pressure, pushing down as hard as I can without exposing the wound completely.

"Why are you doing this?" he whispers, his voice barely audible.

"Because you're messing up, Will. You're making one mistake after another, and I want to help you."

"You don't even know what you're talking about," he snaps.

A lieutenant and a few deputies walk by, nodding in our direction. We plaster smiles on our faces, pretending to be just two colleagues shooting the breeze, nothing to see here. Except, of course, there is.

There are cameras around here everywhere. I look up at one, no sound, but some talented people know how to read lips. This is a terrible place to talk. Will knows it as well as I do.

"Let's get some more coffee," he says.

I follow him out to the park. This time, however, we don't make it all the way to the pond, just to the parking lot, just out of shot of any prying ears.

I take a step away, folding my arms across my chest. Will looks down at the ground and slowly back up at me.

"You're not going to let this go, are you?"

"Like I said before, I'm your friend. I want to help you."

"This is going to put you in an impossible situation, Charlotte. You're going to hate me for this."

"Is me knowing going to help?" I ask.

"I don't even know. I have no idea." He shakes his head and gives a fateful shrug, full of fatalism.

"You really don't want to tell me?" I ask, pressing again. Will this be my last time?

"I want to tell you, more than anything," Will insists. "Of course, I do. I need your help. I need to have someone to run all of this by. But then you'll be part of it. And I don't know what to do about that."

"Are you sleeping with Erin Lowry?" I ask again.

He takes a deep breath.

"I did. Remember that woman I told you about, the love of my life, the one who got away in college? That's *her*."

"That's *her*?" My mouth drops open.

"I had no idea that she was living here. Then I ran into her once, before all of this happened, at a bar. We kissed. We almost let it go too far. It was a couple of weeks before the murders. I didn't get her number. I tried to find her, but she told me she didn't want to be found. And then the next time I saw her was in the interrogation room after she was suspected of murdering her husband, his new wife, and unborn child. I couldn't believe it."

“So, you helped her?" I whisper.

”No. I tried to be as professional as I could. I mean, I was shocked and I didn't tell you. And I didn't tell the lieutenant, of course. But I didn't do anything to help Erin specifically. This whole time I've just been trying to figure out what really happened, how to make any of this make any sense."

“I'm so sorry, Will," I say, dropping my arms to my sides and then bringing them around him for a hug. "I'm so sorry that you're dealing with this."

"I kept wanting to tell you, Charlotte. I knew that you, of all people, would understand. But I didn't want to bring you in on it. Every time we talked to her, every time we went further with this case, the more improper my conduct became. I should have just come forward. But I wanted to see if she had anything to do with this. I don't know… I guess I wanted to find out the truth."

"That's what we're doing though, right?"

"Yeah. But I didn't want to be taken off the case. And I would have been. You know that."

"That would've been the right thing to do," I say.

He shrugs.

"It just got so convoluted. I thought I'd wait until the gun residue and toxicology tests came back. And now that she's probably going to be arrested, I don't know. This is why I couldn't tell you the truth. I already made so many mistakes and I didn't want to bring you in on this. What are you going to do?"

I bite my lower lip, a nervous habit that I've had for a long time.

"You have to tell the lieutenant," I say.

Will forces a smile. He looks at me with big soulful eyes, as if I have all the answers in the world. I don't.

He's right about everything, telling me the truth has put me in the middle of an impossible situation. The right thing to do is to tell the lieutenant immediately and get Will off the case. But that will open an internal affairs investigation. They probably won't let me stay on this case either and another set of detectives will be assigned, with different approaches and investigative techniques.

Like him, I don't want to give up this case. Like him, I want to get to the truth.

"Do you think Erin had anything to do with this?" I ask.

He shakes his head no.

"I don't believe you. You wouldn't be fighting so hard if you thought she were innocent," I challenge him.

"You think I'd fight harder if I thought she was guilty of killing an unborn child?"

"I don't know. Probably not. But you love her. You're trying to protect her for what you didn't do back then."

"I am," Will admits. "I made a lot of mistakes and I have a lot of regrets. I know that Erin looks guilty as hell, but I don't feel it. I know that we're here to make a case for the prosecution. That double murder, possible triple murder, can't go unpunished. But I don't think Erin did it. I don't have any proof, except that she called the police. She was disoriented, lost."

"The toxicology report should be back soon," I say.

He nods his head. "Yeah. I'm waiting on that, too. Erin says that she can't remember. And I believe her. Maybe I'm an idiot."

"Yeah, maybe you are," I say.

"You think that all I see is the woman that I used to love?"

I shift my weight from one foot to another, cross my arms again, and look at him more discerningly.

"I think your love for her and everything that you used to feel for her is blinding you as to what's real."

He swallows hard.

"Maybe. But will you give me the benefit of the doubt?"

"That's what I'm doing here, Will. That's why I'm still here. That's why I'm not sure if I should go to the lieutenant now..."

"You should," Will says. "You should go to the lieutenant now. But know that it's going to get us both off the case. What then? Nielsen and Ramon will be assigned. And you know how they are, how quick on the trigger, even not beyond planting evidence to get a conviction."

"That's a rumor," I point out.

"Yeah, but it's that convenient thing that tends to happen, right? If they're assigned to the case, I doubt we'll ever find out the truth. We'll always have doubts about whether Erin actually did it or not."

I nod, biting my lower lip once again. He's right about everything. But what can I do?

33

ERIN

As soon as Detective Pierce leaves, I close the door behind her and continue gripping onto the doorknob without moving away. My anxiety is through the roof. My heart is stomping out of my chest. I can't catch my breath, and I can't make myself move.

Just take your hand off the doorknob, I say silently to myself to prompt my body into action, without much success.

I continue to grip on, my knuckles turning white, my face leaning against the door frame, inhaling the sweet scent of old acrylic paint and wood.

"It's going to be fine. It's going to be fine," I finally speak the words out loud, but I don't believe them anymore than I did when I said them silently.

She saw *Will* here. She saw how flustered and odd he was.

She called me on the positive GSR test, the proof that I was there, or at least that I shot the gun.

Why else would the residue be on my hands?

What possible other explanation could there be?

A part of me is surprised that she didn't arrest me right on the spot, but they probably don't think I'm a flight risk, and they're just trying to put all their ducks in a row.

I pry my hand off the doorknob and run upstairs to the master bedroom. Opening the closet door, I grab the suitcase and start stuffing clothes inside.

Run.

Run is all I can do right now.

I'll run away and go somewhere where no one knows my name and no one knows this terrible thing that I have done.

"But I didn't do anything," I say, scooping up my panties, bras, and socks and tossing them into the bag. In the drawer below, I find my most comfortable clothes: crew neck t-shirts, hoodies. When I try to zip the suitcase, it's bursting at the seams. Nothing is folded and it's a tight fit, but I don't care. I need to get out of here.

They're not going to arrest me for something I didn't do.

Or did I?

The GSR test is positive. I hear Detective Pierce's words in my head on a loop.

I touched the gun.

I shot it.

I did that terrible thing to Derek that I threatened to do all of this time and never thought that I would have the courage.

Is that what it is, or is it desperation?

I'm so pathetic. This whole story is pathetic: a jilted ex-wife who can't possibly understand that her marriage is over.

The husband took off with someone else. He cheated. So what? It's so banal. It has happened to millions of people around the world.

For some reason, people want to move on prior to making the leap. They want to have another ship to jump onto, another relationship to lose themselves in rather than jumping into the deep blue ocean with no life raft.

I've had those urges myself; men that I found attractive, men that I could imagine being with, but I never did because I thought we had something special. This isn't even about Derek. I'm not even jealous about him anymore.

Yeah, because he's dead, I say to myself. You got what you wanted.

I'm arguing with a phantom, a figment of my imagination. Yet, no matter how much I search my mind, I can't remember handling a weapon. Or shooting one.

As far as Susannah is concerned, I would have never shot her *while* she was pregnant.

But maybe I did. Who knows?

Tears flow down my cheeks, and I wipe them with the back of my hands. The suitcase is heavy, hard to carry downstairs, and it bounces loudly from side to side.

"They're going to arrest me. I have to do this," I say, looking at myself in the mirror in the foyer. My face is drenched, makeup soaked, my eyes splotched and red. I have stains underneath my arms from sweating so much from all the anxiety, despair, and confusion.

Where will I go?

Just get in the car, I say to myself. Just get in the car and drive. You have your license. You have your money. You can withdraw some cash on the way. You can do this. You *have* to do this to save yourself.

But wouldn't I look even more guilty?

It doesn't matter. They won't be able to find you. You'll live on the run. You'll stay in cheap hotels, but you'll make a new life away from here, and if they find you, well, at least you gave it a shot. You didn't just walk yourself to the slaughter. You fought the good fight.

I toss my suitcase in the trunk, start the engine. My mind is torn. I'm scared, alone. I want to call Sandra, but I can't. She'll tell me to turn around. She'll tell me that the law can protect me, but that will be a lie. The law can only do so much. The evidence is piling up. I drive off, looking only once in the rearview mirror at the house that I called my home.

"It'll be better this way," I say as I get closer and closer to the freeway.

Signs appear I-10 East, I-10 West.

West goes three hours to Los Angeles and dead ends in the Pacific Ocean. East goes all the way to Florida, but I don't think I'll go that far.

I'll head to Eastern California, maybe take a hard left and lose myself in the desert lands of Arizona and Nevada where there are miles and miles between people.

I can get a new name. These are not the towns east of the Mississippi, which are populated by people who never leave. These are western towns populated by the lost souls, the transients, the people that come and go in search of family, of friends, of a new life. I can start over there.

Soon I see the sign for Blythe, a border town in between California and Arizona that's about 100 miles away. I drive for close to an hour, my mind going blank. Something about the lull of the engine on the freeway pulls me out of the anxiety of the what-ifs.

And then just like that, without any further rumination, I take the nearest exit and get on the road back. If I leave for good, I'm going to do so in a planned and efficient manner. I'm going to prepare. I'm going to get cash. I'm going to pack exactly what I need. I'm not going to run in fear.

With the miles whizzing by, I become more and more certain of my decision. I owe it to myself and to Derek to find out who did this to him and his family.

I don't think it's me, and I shouldn't have to pay the price.

But what if it is?

34

ERIN

When I get back home, I throw the suitcase in the walk-in closet, change my clothes into something more professional, brush my hair and wash my face, reapplying makeup to match the look to my attire. This is my war paint.

If they think that I did this, they're going to have a heck of a time proving it. I'm going to stop being this sad, pathetic girl and I'm going to stand up for myself. They won't be able to pin this on me. They're going to have to really prove it. And if they do, and I did do this, then I'm going to take off, but it's going to be with a plan.

I put on a skirt, pantyhose, high heels, pulling my hair into a low ponytail. It doesn't feel right. The skirt is too feminine. I have not worn one in years and I have to feel comfortable. I change into a pair of slacks, a comfortable pair of flats, and a jacket to match.

“Yes, this is good,” I say, giving myself a glance over. “This is the way to go."

I head to the courthouse where Sandra texted that she would be; we have a lot to talk about and she really needs to make me feel like she's fighting for me.

I know she's a good attorney, but I also know that she has doubts. She says that's not important, but it's not good enough. She's not the kind of person who can fight well with doubt. And I'm not going to put up with anything but the best. No one else is going to fight for me the way that I will and the way that I deserve to be fought for.

So, it's time for me to stop feeling sorry for myself, and to give it a real try to be the attorney that I always was for everyone else. I deserve it.

When I spot Sandra outside the courthouse, she’s grasping onto a bright pink scarf as it twirls around in the wind, threatening to take off. A gust blows my hair in my face.

“It’s so windy out there,” she says, pushing her fingers into her hair and giving herself a once-over in the foyer mirror.

We decide to go back into the courthouse and just get coffee at the Starbucks.

"Thanks for meeting me. I just wanted to talk about the GSR results. Detective Pierce just stopped by my house," I say, shifting my weight from one foot to another. I don't mention Will. I will keep that to myself for now, but I wonder if I should.

"Yes, I meant to come talk to you about that. It came back positive."

I wait for her to explain, to make me feel better. But instead, she just narrows her eyes and waits for me to say something.

"What does this mean exactly?" I ask.

"It means that the person touched the gun that was fired or was there when it was fired."

"But I wasn't in the vicinity. And I didn't handle any gun." I play with the paper sleeve around the cup.

"But are you sure about that? I mean, how do you know for sure?"

"I know because I know!"

"Erin, I'm not trying to be…cruel." It takes her a few moments to find the right word and that's not lost on me.

"But you say that you don't remember being there and yet you were. You called the police. What if you did something *before* you called them? Isn't it possible?"

"Yes, of course it's possible. Anything is possible," I start to say.

"Well, then?"

Sandra narrows her eyes again. This look. I hate it. It makes me feel very small. I've seen her give this look to her kids on more than one occasion.

"Who do you think you are, Sandra?" I ask after a moment. She inhales deeply, uncertain if I had actually uttered these words. But I'm more certain than I ever was before.

"You are my attorney, but you don't have to be. That is if you don't believe me. I have plenty of people second-guessing me. The last thing I need is you doing the same thing."

"Erin, that's not what I'm doing."

"Oh, yeah? Because that's exactly what it sounds like to me."

"Me, too," a rich deep voice says from the stairwell. Just hearing these two words makes my whole body shiver.

"Christopher?" Sandra asks. His name comes out slowly as if the ground under her feet were shaking and she only now realized it.

"Hi, Sandy," he says, leaning against the wall and biting into an apple.

It's a public place in the courthouse, a space where people gather to take a breather or grab a quick lunch. All the tables are taken, voices are echoing all around, but then everyone except the three of us ceases to exist.

"My name is Sandra. You know that."

"All I know is that you prefer Sandra. But that might just be because you are pretentious," Christopher says, taking another huge bite out of the apple. "Fine, let's go with Sandra. Why is it that *you* are interrogating Erin? Wasn't she clear with you about her not remembering anything?"

I both hate and love him for standing up to her. She is my friend, but it's nice to have someone really on my side.

"You are such a dick," she says and then turns to me. "Erin, I didn't mean anything by what I said. I mean, anything offensive. All I meant is that is there any possibility that you might be…confused? Perhaps, something did happen and you just…"

"Don't remember?" I fill in the blank. "Yes, I don't. I already told you that."

"So, why did the GSR come back positive?"

"As you know, Sandra, the GSR results can come back positive for a variety of reasons. It could mean that she handled the gun or was in the vicinity of a gun when it was fired, but it could also mean that she touched something that was around the gun when it was fired.

Didn't you tell me that you touched Susannah's body?"

"Yes, I did! I did." I get a little bit too excited perhaps, but at this point I'd grab onto anything that doesn't make me feel like I'm going crazy.

"Well, that's it then," Christopher says. "When you checked on her, some GSR particles must've transferred over."

I glare at Sandra who doesn't have a good rebuttal. She simply stares at me and shakes her head.

"Isn't that possible?" I ask. "Are you so certain that I did it?"

Does she really not believe me? Isn't she my friend?

Why is she questioning me like this? I want to go over there and shake her, but I keep my hands to myself.

"I'm sorry, Erin. I'm not certain of anything. I'm just here asking you questions. These are the kind of questions that the cops will ask you."

That sentence makes my blood run cold.

"These are the types of questions that the prosecution is going ask you," she adds.

Is going to ask me? Present tense. She doesn't clarify that statement. It's a matter of fact. No, no, no. Thoughts rush through my mind a mile a minute. She doesn't believe me. She says she does, but she doesn't.

"I know that this is difficult, Erin. But I have to ask you these questions and you have to answer them. I can only put the cops off for so long."

"Let me ask you a question. What does a negative result mean, Sandra?" Christopher butts in.

"It can mean a number of things," Sandra says with a definitive shrug. "Like the person was nowhere near the gun when it was fired."

"Yes, and what else?"

"I don't know, Christopher. Why don't you enlighten me?"

"Why don't I?" he says with the cocky smile of a television lawyer. This must be the expression that the jury sees, almost always making them side with him.

"A negative GSR result might also mean that the person was near but not close enough for GSR to land on them. Or it can mean that the GSR deposited on them wore off."

"And your point is?"

"My point is that as much as cops want to make of GSR, the results don't really tell you much about who was or wasn't at the crime scene. Besides the fact that GSR only stays on hands for about four to six hours, it can also be wiped off very easily. A person can wipe off GSR by just sticking his or her hands in and out of their pockets."

"So what?"

"GSR results, whether they are positive or negative, don't really mean crap. For Christ's sake, even suicide victims who shot themselves can test negative for GSR. And if you were a lawyer worth your shit, you would know that."

"I do know that."

"You do?" I ask.

"Of course, I do, Erin."

"So, why are you here, making such a big deal out of this?"

"Because test results aren't just whether they prove or disprove something, Erin. They're also about the truth. I came here to ask you if you…did…"

"You came here to accuse your client of murder?" Christopher interrupts again, saying exactly what's on my mind.

"Don't you remember the first rule of being a lawyer, Sandra? It doesn't matter whether your client did it or not. What matters is if they can prove it."

"I didn't come to talk to you as your lawyer, Erin," Sandra says, ignoring him. Christopher is driving her up a wall and she's about to break.

Yet, she manages to stay calm. "I came here to talk to you as a friend, who really cares about you."

"Honestly, it doesn't feel like that. It feels like you are accusing me of killing Derek and Susannah and the baby! Do you honestly think I'm capable of something like that?"

"You don't know what happened, Erin. You said so yourself."

She's pivoting. Avoiding my question. I look deep into her eyes and, there, I see it.

She's having doubts. At first, she supported me because she thought that I didn't do it.

But now? Now, she's doing it because she's my friend. Well, that's not enough.

"I need you to leave, Sandra," I say after a moment.

"What?"

I repeat myself and walk back to the courthouse.

"I'm going to call you later when you are feeling more like yourself," Sandra threatens.

"There's no need."

"What? Why?"

"Sandra, I need an attorney who believes me. Someone who doesn't second-guess me at every turn."

"I do. I do believe you, Erin," she pleads.

"No, you don't. You don't. And that's okay. I know that my story is…unusual. But I'm trying to get to the bottom of it. To figure out what really happened because the one thing that I know for sure is that I didn't do it."

"Erin, please—" Sandra starts to say but I usher her out.

"If you can't convince me that you believe in me, how are you going to convince the cops? Or the prosecutor? Or God forbid, the jury?"

35

ERIN

Sandra calls me later that day but I don't answer. I can't talk to her. I don't know how the whole day started off so wrong. Why did Detective Pierce have to come by? Why did Sandra have to accuse me of things I know that she knows I didn't do?

She calls my phone over and over. I keep letting it go to voice mail. I ignore all of her texts. She is sorry for saying those things, but what if she isn't sure about my innocence? Can I really have someone representing me who has doubts?

My thoughts return to last night. Will's lips on my collarbone. His hands on my back. Shivers run down my spine and goose bumps appear on my arms. I take a shower to try to get him out of my head without much success.

I would never let myself admit it but I don't think I ever stopped loving him. We fit so well together in college.

We just got each other and never had any of the growing pains of a new relationship, the complete opposite of Derek and me.

Sandra leaves me another voice mail.

"Erin, please, you have to call me," she pleads. This time I decide to call her back.

"What do you want?" I ask.

She apologizes profusely about everything that she said this morning and I begrudgingly accept her apology. But right before she hangs up, she brings up Christopher.

"He is not the person you think he is," she says. "I just want you to be careful."

"What are you talking about?"

"There is just something…untrustworthy about him, Erin. I think he's pretending to be your friend."

"No, he's not. Why would he? He was one of Derek's closest friends."

"I don't know, but I just don't trust him," Sandra says after a moment.

That's it. I've had enough of this.

"Sandra, what the hell happened between you two? Why do you hate him so much?"

She pauses for a while. I wait.

"He is not a very honorable person. Not a very trustworthy attorney. He was always taking shortcuts. One of the reasons that I left was that he took a client that I didn't think we should have been representing."

"What client?"

"A shady businessman who paid his legal bills from a numbered account from Bermuda. He supposedly ran a restaurant here in town, but we all suspected him to be laundering money. Actually, we knew for sure that they were laundering money since he admitted as much to Christopher."

"And what did Christopher say?"

"He didn't seem to be bothered by it. I mean, he paid some lip service to how this is a client we need to be careful about, blah, blah, blah, but in the end, he was the one who had convinced Derek to take him on."

"And Derek didn't want to?"

"He had his hesitations."

It's times like these that I hate the formal language that attorneys tend to fall back on when they tell you things that they don't really want to say. Sandra is no stranger to that. Derek had his hesitations really means that he wasn't into it until Christopher won him over with the promise of a big pay day.

"This is all confidential, of course. You're not supposed to know this," Sandra says. "I'm just telling you to warn you about him. That's why I left that firm. When I first started, it was a pretty honorable place to work. We fought for clients we believed in. We made money but it wasn't all about the money. It was about doing the right thing. And now…well, ever since the other partner left and it's pretty much all Christopher's game now, things have changed…things are completely different."

"How did Derek feel about this?" I ask.

"Honestly, I don't know. We were never very close and after I left, we didn't really stay in touch."

I nod.

"So, you're not going to see him again, right?" Sandra asks, her voice going up at the end. She catches me so off guard, I pull the phone away from me and take a step back.

"What?"

She repeats her question.

"Are you seriously asking me this?" I ask, shaking my head.

"I thought you understood. Christopher is only out for himself. He's not someone you want to be involved with right now."

"Who do you think you are, Sandra?"

"I'm your attorney. Everything you do now is under a microscope."

"Well, good, because I'm not doing anything suspicious."

"Your husband had an affair, married his girlfriend, and was expecting a child with her. He was also married to someone else while he was married to you. And now he's dead," she says.

"But not as a result of anything that I did."

"You found their bodies, Erin. You have no good explanation for being at their home in the middle of the night."

"But I didn't kill anyone."

"I know that, but the GSR test came back positive—" she starts to say.

"No, I don't think you do. I think you think that I did it, Sandra. You don't believe me," I interrupt her.

Now, it's her to turn to listen. I tell her everything that's on my mind. I unload and don't hold back. And in the end, I tell her that I don't think I need someone representing me who doesn't believe me.

"Lawyers like to say that it doesn't matter whether or not their clients did it. All that matters is if they can prove that they didn't. But you're not one of those lawyers, Sandra. You only represent clients you *believe* in. So, let me do *you* a favor. I'm going to let you go."

"You're firing me?"

"Yes," I say and hang up.

That wasn't exactly how I had planned for that to go. I didn't want to lose Sandra as a lawyer or a friend. She's really good and reliable. And she works hard.

But the words that spilled out were the truth. She isn't the type to represent anyone she doesn't whole heartedly believe in, and I can't be her test case.

I have way too much on the line for this.

I find Christopher's number in my phone and shoot him a text.

I NEED A LAWYER.

36

ERIN

A few days later, I arrive at the police station for our scheduled sit down with Detective Pierce. She sells it as a meeting to let me know how the case is going and to update me about what is going on. Though, we both know very well that cops do not update potential murder suspects about cases that they're working on.

Detective Pierce is friendly and cordial when I arrive, showing me to a meeting room with windows. This must be where they take people who they are trying to butter up. Either that or people with expensive lawyers they know they can't get over on so easily.

Many attorneys I've worked with absolutely hate cops, even the ones who have never come in contact with them because they primarily do civil litigation.

I can hear my criminal law professor's voice in my head, "Cops will do just about anything to make their case, not withstanding, breaking some laws and infringing on the constitutional rights of suspects. And the ones who are even less scrupulous? Well, they'll just go out there and lie and cheat and frame anyone they think did it if it gets their cases closed."

When she pours me a cup of coffee from the breakfast cart at the far end of the room, I look Detective Pierce up and down and wonder what kind of police officer she is.

Is she the type to do just about anything to get her suspect locked up or is she someone who toes the line? Judging from the fact that she is pretty young to be a detective, I get the feeling that she has broken a few laws in order to get her shield.

"You don't like cops, do you?" she asks, sitting down at the table.

I shrug and bite into my muffin.

"About as much as I like lawyers," I say with a smile.

"Given that you are no longer one, I guess that's not much of a compliment."

"No, I was just kidding," I backtrack.

"It's okay. I'm not in this job for popularity."

"And I'm actually going back to work soon. At my old firm."

"Oh, really? Derek's firm?"

"That's where I worked, too, before I got pregnant. Christopher said there was an opening. And I need to do something…productive."

"I'm sorry again about your miscarriages," she says, putting her hand on mine. "I know how hard that can be."

"I appreciate it," I say dismissively.

The cynical part of me wants to believe that she's just saying these things to form a connection with me. She is just pretending to be my friend so that I will open up to her. But sitting here, with her hand squeezing mine softly, I feel like it's something more.

"Have you ever had one?" I ask.

"No." She shakes her head.

"Then you don't know what I'm talking about."

"I agree." She nods.

We both stare into space, somewhere a little past each other.

"So, why did you ask me here?" I ask after a moment. I'm eager to change the topic. Sharing this dark part of my life doesn't change anything between us. At least, I don't want it to.

"Well, as you know, the GSR test came back positive."

I inhale and breathe out slowly, trying to buy some time.

"Do want to wait for Ms. Pullman before answering my questions?"

"She's not my attorney anymore."

"Really?"

"Yes, we had a bit of a disagreement. I'm now represented by Christopher Flynn."

She stares at me with a dumbfound look on her face.

"Isn't he a partner at your ex-husband's firm?"

"Yes. My old firm."

"And this isn't a conflict of interest for him?"

"Sandra worked there, too."

"But she didn't for a long time. Mr. Flynn was working with Derek when he was killed."

"It's a big firm with lots of lawyers. He's a friend of mine. Besides, I don't really see how this is any of your concern. As long as he has an active license, I can hire whomever I want."

"Yes, you can, of course." Detective Pierce waves her hand. "So, would you like to wait for Mr. Flynn before starting?"

I glance at the clock. I've been here for thirty-five minutes already. Perfect. He's not only late, but *very* late. It's not like I have anywhere to be, but no one wants to stay in a police station longer than necessary.

“No, I have things to do,” I say. “Let’s talk now.”

Detective Pierce asks me about the GSR results and why they could’ve came back positive. I parrot back what I heard Christopher say to Sandra, which seems to shut down this line of questioning, at least for now.

Detective Pierce seems to be satisfied with my answers as to why the GSR results came back positive and doesn’t bring it up again. So, I ask about the gun that they found. She’s surprised and does not come forward with anything more than what I have already heard from Sandra. They found a gun. They don’t know who it belongs to. They are running more tests.

I’ve never practiced criminal law, but I’ve seen people do it. What they don’t show you on television and in movies is exactly how much time passes between when they find evidence and when they are finished with all the tests. Obviously, it doesn’t take an hour, but it also doesn’t take a week. Most likely, it’s a month or more. It all depends on what lab they use and how backed up that lab is with things to test.

“So, I was thinking something. Maybe it was one of Derek’s disgruntled clients,” I offer.

“We’ve looked into that.”

“And?”

“Well, he did have a disgruntled client,” she admits.

"Really?" My heart skips a beat. I lean in closer to her with anticipation.

"Derek represented a client in a real estate deal that went sour. They lost and the client had to pay his partner a lot of money."

I have not heard about this before, but then again I haven't been in Derek's life for a long time.

"The client made a lot of threats against him afterward."

"Okay, so, maybe it was him who did it."

"Not possible," Detective Pierce says, shaking her head.

"He's got an alibi."

"What kind?"

"One that's unbreakable. He was on a flight at the time of the murders."

I shake my head.

"We checked it out, Erin. Checked the flight records. Saw him on the video footage. He didn't do it."

"Except that you don't know *exactly* when this happened, right?"

She inhales deeply. "Erin, I'm not here to explain our procedures to you. I probably shouldn't have even told you this much."

"Why did you?"

"Because…because…I'm getting pressured to close this case. More tests are going to come in soon and I want to give you a chance to explain yourself."

She stares into my eyes, searching for answers that I can't give her.

There's a knock on the door and the person doesn't wait for permission to step inside.

"Now, Detective Pierce, you are not asking my client any questions without her attorney's presence, are you?"

"This is just a friendly chat. She's not under arrest. And she was more than willing to talk."

"I'm sorry I'm late," Christopher whispers to me as he sits down. I glare at him, but keep my mouth shut.
For now.

"So, what did I miss?"

37

ERIN

As Christopher helps himself to some coffee, Detective Pierce fills him in on what we talked about. He asks her a bit more about this disgruntled client who had threatened Derek, but she doesn't give him any more information than she has given me.

"So, another thing that I wanted to talk to you about," Detective Pierce pivots the conversation. "Maura."

The name sends shivers up my spine. It hangs in mid-air between us as if it's a word bubble in a comic strip. Christopher looks at us blankly.

"Maura Foley," Detective Pierce clarifies as if any of us know of another Maura.

"Oh, yes, Derek's first wife. Or should we call her the *main* wife? Since he was still married to her when he and my client divorced," Christopher says.

We did it in a court of law but no one at the time, except for Derek, knew that the whole thing was a sham. We were never married. We never needed to get divorced.

"I don't care what you call her," Detective Pierce says, looking straight at me. "All I want to know is *why* did you go see *her*?"

All the blood rushes away from my face and pools somewhere in between my toes. I feel faint, but I pretend that I'm fine.

Nothing is wrong. Not at all.

"You did go to see her, right?" Detective Pierce asks.

She's leaning closer to me, invading my personal space with abandon. The regretful expression on her face, the one that made it clear that she was sorry that she hadn't brought up Maura earlier, before my lawyer got here, is all but gone.

"I—" I start to say, but Christopher presses his hand on mine.

"I am advising my client not to answer this question."

"Why not?"

"I don't really need a reason. But if you insist. We are here answering your questions as a courtesy. We are here out of the goodness of our hearts."

"You've never done anything out of the goodness of your heart."

"Nevertheless. Erin doesn't have to answer any questions that she doesn't want to or that I advise her not to answer. And I do not want her answering this one."

"Now, isn't that suspicious?" Detective Pierce narrows her eyes, looking past him and directly at me.

Christopher shrugs and leans back in his chair. If this occasion wasn't so formal, I'm sure that he would put his hands above his head and interlock his fingers, while balancing on the two back legs of his chair. You know, like the popular guys do in high school.

"Actually, come to think of it, I think we're done here,' he adds. 'You aren't offering us any new information on my client's ex-husband's brutal murder and we don't like the tone that you are taking here. Erin had nothing to do with this and you and I both know it."

His certainty is disarming. I'm actually shocked and taken aback. We say brief goodbyes and I follow him out of the building.

"You know, I was so mad at you for coming late, but now…you definitely made up for it."

"What the hell was that, Erin?" He turns around, glaring at me.

"What?"

"You went to Maura's house? They have proof of you being there? What the hell were you doing there? And why didn't you tell me?"

"I don't know how they could've found out."

"They're cops. They find stuff out," he says, fuming. "What happened?"

I take a deep breath and tell him everything. He listens carefully, shaking his head.

"I still have no idea how they could've found out," I say.

"Some neighbor might have seen them. Or she might have told them about some weirdo she saw lurking on her street."

"I'm not a weirdo."

"I know that." His voice softens a bit. "But you still can't do that. And the other thing that you can't do is confirm anything. If this goes anywhere, if this goes to trial, they have to fight us on every bit of evidence. We can't just have you confirming that you did in fact talk to Maura Foley. If they want to tell the jury that and have them believe it, then they will have to prove it. And it will be our word against theirs."

He's right. Of course, he's right. He's Christopher Flynn. He's always right. I hate this, but it's true. I let out a deep breath. I'm so glad that he was there today, stopping me from being my own worst enemy. This knight in shining armor is a good look for him.

I'm tempted to tell him about Will, but I'm afraid of his reaction.

"What did you tell them before I got there?"

"Nothing."

"Erin," he says, using the tone that someone would use to scold a child.

"Why were you late? You knew what time the meeting was."

"I had court. But you didn't have to go in and talk to her. You could've waited."

"I'm your client. I didn't want to be there all day."

"You have nothing to do, Erin. The least you can do is not put yourself on trial for murder."

I hate the tone of his voice. I hate how he is telling me what to do. Why is he so angry?

38

ERIN

Large heavy drops bounce against my windshield as I drive to Shawn Nieves' office. I should have just called him, but I couldn't find his card or his info anywhere. When I tried to look him up on Google, I couldn't find anything either.

What kind of private investigator doesn't have anything about his business online? How are people supposed to find him? I couldn't very well call Sandra, so here I am going to see him in person.

Given the fact that I survived law school and once made a living as an attorney, I'm actually surprisingly bad at in-person confrontations. Whenever possible, I prefer to discuss unpleasant things through the phone, or better yet, through email or a text. There's something about delivering bad news in person that is particularly unappealing and uncomfortable.

The parking lot in front of his shabby office is filled to the brim and I drive around for a bit waiting for a spot to open up. What are all these people doing here? Are they all getting food at the Chinese buffet at the far end of the strip or is there some kind of dental emergency plaguing the people of Palm Valley?

After a good ten minutes of driving around the parking lot, I press on the brake and stop in the middle of the lane. There's no one in front of me or behind me. I watch as the windshield wipers fling around from one side to the other of my rental car.

This rental has already cost me close to one thousand dollars and who knows how much more it's going to be. I should've asked Detective Pierce when I'll be able to get my car back from impound, but I forgot. Now, I'll have to have another interaction, another opportunity for her to make me feel like their number one suspect in their open, double murder case. Or is it a triple murder case now? She mentioned something about the district attorney looking into classifying it as such given that the baby was healthy and more than six months in utero.

No, no, I can't think about this now. My head starts to throb. The sound of each droplet colliding against my windshield makes it worse. I'm just not going to think about it anymore. That's all. I mean, you can't do anything to change it, so why worry about it, right?

Or better yet, why not let Christopher, your new attorney, deal with getting your car back? Yes, of course. That's what I'll do.

A woman comes out of the nail salon by Shawn's office. Wrestling with her unyielding umbrella, she jogs across the parking lot to her car, which is luckily parked right to the left of me. I pull back a bit to let her out and then take her spot. I look for some Advil in my purse and find a loose pill at the bottom. It's covered in some sort of fluff, but I'm in no position to be picky. I pop the pill into my mouth and wash it down with a generous amount of water.

I don't have an umbrella. I didn't park far from his office, but I still get soaked on my run over there. Knocking on his door, I stomp my feet and swish some of the water off my coat.

"Come in!" he yells through the door.

I take a deep breath before going inside. At first, I don't see him. There's no one in the main room. But looking down the dark hallway, I see that there's another smaller room back there.

"Shawn?"

"I'm back here."

The last thing I want to do right now is to walk back there into his private space, so I just stay put.

"Are you coming?" he yells out.

"Um…okay," I mumble.

I walk around the desk up front and head down the hallway. I find him lying on a cot, dressed in dark jeans, a plain white t-shirt, and hiking boots. He's holding a small paperback book in front of his face and doesn't look up until I clear my throat.

"Oh, hey. Erin, right?" He sits up.

"I'm sorry to bother you," I say. "I lost your card. And I wanted to tell you that I won't need your services anymore."

"Really? They arrested someone?"

"What?"

"Did the police arrest someone in your ex-husband's murder?"

I give him a blank stare.

"No," I say slowly.

"I don't understand."

"Well, I decided to go with another lawyer. Sandra isn't going to be representing me anymore."

"Why is that?"

I'm about to delve into it, but then something occurs to me. "It's really none of your business."

"Fine."

"Listen, I don't want to be rude. I just lost your card and I couldn't find you online anywhere. So, I'm here telling you that I'm good. Thanks for all of your help and all. I'll see you around."

I really hope that I don't. There's this disarming way that he looks at me that makes me very uncomfortable. If I were pressed on the issue, and if I were still drinking, I'd have to admit that the feeling is not entirely bad. That look of his makes me feel like he can see through all of my crap, down to the core of who I really am.

I turn around and start to walk back to the front door. I feel his gaze burning into my back.

"What do you know about Maura Foley?" Shawn yells out right before I get outside.

"What?" I ask, keeping the door open. Rain drizzles onto my arm, pooling in the crevices.

He says something I can't quite make out.

"Maura Foley," Shawn says, coming out of the back room. "What do you know about her?"

THAT NAME MAKES me stop dead in my tracks. I don't want to turn around. I take a moment to collect my thoughts.

"I know that you went to see her. And that the cops know that, too," Shawn informs me.

Shivers run down my spine. How could he possibly know that?

"I know because I'm good at my job, Erin," he says, as if he is able to read my mind.

"So, what?" I ask after a moment. "So, what if I did?"

"It wasn't wise."

I shrug.

"You went to her and you told her who you were."

"No, I didn't."

"She figured it out."

I shake my head and turn toward the door. I don't have to listen to this.

"My source says you're their primary suspect, but it doesn't have to be that way."

"What are you talking about?"

"Are you firing me?"

I take a step back. "I don't know you. Don't you work for Sandra?"

"No, I work for you. I'm on your case. No matter who your attorney is."

"Okay," I mumble, at a loss.

On one hand, he must be very good at his job. He knows a lot about what's going on with this case, information that I have no idea how he could possibly have. Yet I'm not sure that I need him anymore. No, that's not true. I do need him.

"I didn't do this," I say to Shawn. "Do you believe me?"

He looks me up and down as if he's carefully considering his answer. "Actually, I do. Against my better judgement."

"What are you talking about?"

"You have no explanation for being there. You supposedly have no memory of what happened and yet you were found wandering around their house."

"I wasn't found. I was there and I called the police."

"And why was that exactly?"

To that, I have no good answer.

"But you did not know about Maura Foley. His first wife. The woman he was still married to when you were married to him. That's a good sign."

"Why is that a good sign?" I gasp.

"Because it makes you look innocent."

"More like ignorant," I correct him.

"You have quite a way with words."

"Well, I wasn't always just a lonely private investigator living in my office, you know," Shawn says with a wink.

"Oh, yeah? What were you before?"

"Sandra didn't tell you? I'm surprised. She is usually so upstanding and upfront about things."

I stare and wait for him for to answer my question.

"I used to be a cop."

"What?" I gasp and put my hand on my throat. Who the hell is this guy and why did Sandra hire him?

"Don't worry. It's not all bad. They didn't fire me for anything illicit. It was all a big misunderstanding."

"Yeah, I'm sure." I roll my eyes.

Police departments are always firing people for completely normal things, I think to myself, but I don't press for more answers. For now.

"So, are you going to tell me what happened?"

I wait for his reply as he fishes around for a file in his desk drawer. When he finally finds it, he opens it on his lap and looks up at me.

"Maybe some other time. Why don't you have a seat?"

Shawn points to the chair in front of the desk and I reluctantly sit down. I don't want to be here. I want to run, but something is forcing me to stay.

"Maura knows that Derek is dead," Shawn says matter of factly.

I stare at him dumbfounded.

"How? Do you think she did it?"

"The cops told her. Frankly, I don't know if she did it. But there is a very strong possibility."

"How do you know this?"

"I've been tracking her movements. I don't know if she knew about you earlier, there's a strong possibility, but she has been looking you up online after you stopped by to see her."

"Oh my God," I whisper. "I'm so stupid. I should've never gone to see her."

"No, you shouldn't have. You should've left it up to me."

I bury my head in my hands.

"What were you thinking?" he asks. I shrug without looking up at him. I shake my head. The problem is that I wasn't thinking. I was just…acting on impulse. Nothing good comes from that.

"My source at the police department tells me that they are looking at both you and her. Since you are his exes."

He runs his finger along the manila folder on his lap. It's my file and it contains everything about my life that's relevant to this case. At least, what Shawn Nieves thinks is relevant.

All the gritty details.

How much of what it contains do I even know?

39

ERIN

Shawn pours me a cup of coffee and offers me some baked goods that he just got from the corner bakery. When I bite into the everything bagel, I remember how Derek was never one to shy away from a grand gesture. He never forgot an anniversary. He always bought me an extravagant bouquet of flowers to commemorate every Valentine's Day.

I remember how sorry I felt for all of those other women who were married to un-romantic guys. You know, the types who never sent any gifts or cards. They were married to suckers, I thought. They were married to men who didn't appreciate them. Men who didn't know how to express themselves.

And now? I wish I had a husband like that. Not only did my hubby have a long affair, but he was married to this woman and was expecting a child with her. Again, that happens to so many women, it's almost banal.

What made Derek a particular kind of ass was that even in our breakup, he went above and beyond what was necessary to hurt me. He made our whole life, our entire love story, one big fat lie.

Because the thing is…we were never really married.

"That must have been very hard to hear," Shawn says, pulling a chocolate croissant apart with his hands. "That your marriage wasn't real."

"Uh-huh." I nod. "You could say that."

"How are you holding up?"

"I just want him out of my life," I blurt out.

My eyes open wider as I realize what I have just said.

"No, sorry, I didn't mean it that way."

"I know exactly what you meant," he says with a lot of compassion. "You just want to stop thinking about him."

"Exactly. Why doesn't anyone else get that?"

We chew silently for a few minutes.

"But now that they're dead, I'm even more intertwined with him than ever. I can't just stop thinking about him, especially when everyone thinks that I was the one who killed them."

"Is that why you went to talk to Maura?" Shawn asks.

I shrug. "Yeah, I guess."

"Erin, please, don't go over there again. I'm serious. No matter what happens."

"But, don't you see? *She* has all the answers. I mean, did she know that he was married to me all this time? Or did he lie to her, too? She had a child. Is it Derek's? I have so many questions…"

My voice trails off as a million thoughts swirl around in my head.

"I don't think she knew," Shawn says after a moment. "But I'm not sure. The cops suspect her in his murder, just like they suspect you. And that's a good thing."

"Why?"

"Why? Are you seriously asking me that?"

I shrug.

"Because as long as she remains one of the primary suspects, then you are off the hook. But if they find out that she has a strong alibi or that she didn't know about him and you and him and Susannah…well, then, that's not good for you."

I know all of these things. Of course, I do. I'm not stupid. Just confused. Dazed. It's good to have someone spell it out for me.

"You have to be careful, Erin," Shawn says, pushing a mini-muffin in my direction. I pick it up and dunk it in my coffee.

"You like them soggy?" he gasps.

"No, I like them moist."

"Whatever floats your boat." He bites into a bagel. Dry. Un-toasted. Without a bit of cream cheese anywhere in sight. Disgusting.

"Why do I have to be careful?"

"The cops are closing in. You need to be extra careful and take more precautions."

I still don't understand.

Shawn spells it out for me.

"If you were anyone else, they would've arrested you already."

"No, they wouldn't have."

"The only reasons they haven't yet is because you're a well-off white woman, you retained a powerful attorney, and they need to have all of their ducks in a row before they come after you."

"But what about Maura?"

"She's one of the ducks they have to get in a row. The only caveat is that she hasn't lawyered up yet. I'm sure she will. Soon."

I shake my head and bite into another mini-muffin.

"I think I know who might have done it, but I need your help."

Shawn stares at me without blinking. Without wasting any more time, I launch into what I know about Derek's ex-client, the disgruntled one who was found guilty of domestic violence and blamed Derek for his conviction.

"Detective Pierce said that he has an alibi, that he was on a flight during the murder. But I was thinking, how do they know this for sure? I mean, they don't know the precise time that Derek and Susannah were killed. Do they?"

"The guy's name is Thomas Grayson," Shawn says without missing a beat. "I've looked into him."

"How did you…" My voice trails off.

"Derek applied for a concealed carry permit a month before his death."

"No, he would never do that." I shake my head. "Derek hates guns."

"Be that as it may. He applied and was granted a restraining order against Thomas Grayson and applied for the permit. This guy called and threatened him a lot. He left messages and Derek was clearly afraid of him."

"Okay, yes," I say. "Then he must've done it."

"Doesn't seem likely." Shawn shakes his head. "They have him boarding a flight out of Palm Valley heading to Vegas."

"But what if the murder didn't happen when they think it happened? But an hour or two earlier. That's possible, right?"

"Anything is possible, of course."

Shawn allows me to hold on to this glimmer of hope.

It's all I have and I have to hold on to it tightly. Because if it weren't Grayson or Maura, the alternative is…unacceptable.

It's not every day that you suspect yourself to be the primary suspect in a triple murder. But as I sit here on a hard plastic chair, I start to wonder.

Did I do it? Could I have done it? Am I capable of something like that?

I don't have any answers. I'd like to think that I am not capable. I'd like to think that I am a confident, completely well-put together woman who did not want her husband dead for leaving her.

But who am I kidding? Of course, I did.

There may be other women out there who could've dealt with it differently, but to me this was total betrayal. We had built a life together, a life that I had actually come to like very much.

I didn't express it out loud, but I loved living in my new suburban house in a cul-de-sac. I liked that everything in my kitchen worked and nothing ever broke like it did back in our *charming* apartment back in Philadelphia. I loved having a beautiful and quiet washer and dryer in my own laundry room, which was the size of our old bedroom. I loved having a dishwasher for the first time ever in my life. I loved having all of these things that people call the 'trappings of success.' They weren't just trappings to me. They were symbols of having arrived.

"Do you know who Paul Mann is?" I ask Shawn when he returns from the bathroom. He looks at me with a blank expression.

"He wrote that Derek and Susannah were together since college."

"So?"

"Well, it was my impression that he had only met her not long ago, not that he'd known her since college. Maybe there's something to that."

"I'll look into it."

I remember walking through a baby boutique with Derek when we first started trying to have one. He held my hand tightly and said that I would make the best mother in the world. I looked into his dark kind eyes and knew that in that moment I was more in love with him than I could ever be. And then, as days turned into months and we finally got pregnant, that feeling only intensified.

So, was all of that a lie? Even at this point, I don't really know. It was either all a lie or he was very good at placing everything in his life into neat, sequestered compartments. I was in one. Susannah was in another one. And then, there was Maura. Where did she fit into it all exactly? And what about her child?

My head starts to hurt thinking about all the things that I should have noticed. Signs that he was a cheating and lying bastard. But to be perfectly honest, there weren't really any. I had no idea that Susannah existed until I surprised him in Philly. And if it weren't for their deaths, I would still not know about Maura.

"It's going to be okay," Shawn says, putting his hand on mine. "I will get to the bottom of this. The cops won't have a case."

I force a smile. I believe him, or at least I want to. But I'm not sure if I can. Maybe the police are right in suspecting me in all of this. I don't have any good explanation for where I was before they were killed or why I was walking through their house.

My only consolation is that I didn't want them dead. I did, earlier, when Derek first left me and moved in with her. But by the time they got engaged, I didn't feel anything toward him anymore. I just wanted to forget that he and I ever existed.

40

CHARLOTTE

Over lunch of tuna and egg salad, my thoughts return to Clara Foster and the girl that I used to know. She had dark brown hair, bangs cut bluntly across her forehead. She was obsessed with Stargate One and was fascinated with Egyptology. Instead of posters of Leonardo DiCaprio, she had The Beatles of whom Ringo was her favorite.

I turn off the YouTube video playing on my phone and get onto the laptop and search for her name. What is she doing now besides inviting practically strangers for get-togethers to dredge up the past?

You would think that this thing that happened would have been your typical teenage secret, maybe a boyfriend that was shared between two friends, unbeknownst to either one of them, but I can only wish for something so benign.

No, what we did that summer is unforgivable, and the more years that have passed, the scarier it is to me that four 12 year olds could do something like that and that our secret would remain a secret all of these years later.

I want to imagine that the reason why I never pursued becoming an FBI agent was because of my father and his insistence on that career, but that's not why. He's right, a part of me is hiding out here.

For years, I worried that our secret would be found out, but the truth is that now, I worry that it never will.

There are so many secrets like this that remain that way for years to come. Law enforcement, web sleuths, journalists, they search for answers, but they don't find any. If a group of friends decides to never talk again, what then?

No one else could know.

No one else could find out, because the secret is safe as long as they choose to keep it that way.

In college, I was friends with Clara on Facebook. She moved to Tallahassee for a while. Her mom had moved there to be with her new boyfriend. But then she came back to Long Beach, California, the same place where I went to middle school.

My dad gave little thought to me transferring schools.

"You'll be fine. You're tough and mature" were his words not mine. So, when he wanted to make his commute easier, we moved to Burbank, north of Los Angeles. That was when he met Sherry and I got a whole new family, two sisters and a brother.

We're closer now, but we went through our growing pains as stepchildren. I felt like the one who was always on the outskirts, the odd duck. Sherry was a good mom and she tried to bring me into the fold as much as she could, but I was a ninth grader, rebellious, annoyed, frustrated that I suddenly had to share a room when for years, I'd had my own.

Looking back, I should have taken it as an opportunity to make closer friends, to not rely on my father so much and realize that he would never really be there for me, while Sherry and my siblings could be the family I always wanted.

But then again, I was a dumb ninth grader who'd just made a terrible mistake and was still looking for ways to make up and make amends for things I had done, knowing full well that I could never truly make amends for any of that.

Clara's address in Long Beach is less than two miles away from the school we attended.

I find her easily and see pictures of her three children, the oldest being thirteen.

"Wow, she had him at 20," I say under my breath.

I scroll through, going years into the past, seeing the happy engagement and wedding photos of her husband who was in the Marines at that time and got deployed to Afghanistan. I see pictures of Donnie, the oldest, and their new house in Southern California, and then 34 Palms, which is a base in the high desert by the national park.

Scrolling through, I try looking at just the important posts, the ones that have a lot of comments and find the one about the divorce with rants about custody. Then nothing for a while about her personal life, except for the kids, since she was probably told by her attorney to stay off social media. And then it's almost like her first husband all but disappeared from her life.

I wonder how involved he is in the kids' lives and what her life is really like. Social media shows carefully curated highlights. The things you choose to post are almost as important as the things you choose not to.

Clara never posts videos of her kids crying, having tantrums, potty training, all the things that I imagine no one wants pictures of when they grow up.

All the bad moments.

For the last few years, her life seemed to move into a nice rhythm.

There's another much simpler wedding to her second husband, who works in informational technology, and their two young children, the last one, only three.

I come to the end of her updates. I find out that over the last year, Clara had a lot of issues with endometriosis, and has her mother living with them.

One of the photos is her and the kids standing in front of the craftsman, a typical home in this area of old Long Beach, full of character and occasional termites. It's less than a couple of miles away from the beach and I can almost smell the salty air of the ocean.

I love the desert, but the ocean still calls to me. I've lived in many areas, and it's been one of my favorites. If it weren't for all the memories and regret, I wonder if I'd still be living there. You don't get much house for the cost, not like in the desert and, I've grown comfortable in my spacious three bedroom, a place with rooms that I hardly use. The property values were going up and it only made sense for us to buy at that time.

Us.

I wasn't always going to be someone who lived alone.

When we did the walk-through, there were two of us. The thought pops into my head the way that thoughts do spontaneously, without permission or consent.

A sudden wave of emotion rushes over me.

I've told myself I wasn't going to do this. I wasn't going to let myself think about it.

I blink a few times trying to keep the tears at bay, and this time it works. I didn't go down the path far enough where they were unstoppable.

I open Facebook Messenger and type in her name.

Hey, Clara. This is Charlotte. I got your invitation.

I click send without finishing the thought. Just as I'm about to continue, she writes me back.

Hey, it's so great to hear from you again.

"Crap," I say to myself. This isn't how it's supposed to go. I'm supposed to send the message and that's it.

I really hope you can make it. I'm doing a little reunion for all of our middle school friends and it wouldn't be the same without you.

Is there a particular reason? I want to ask.

I'm not sure if I'll be able to, I type.

I really hope you can, she says. *I'd love to see what you're all up to, and I'm sure you'd like to catch up with all of us as well.*

She is definitely adding some pressure. I'm tempted to ask who's coming, wanting to know that if this is some special conversation about what happened or the invitation's extended to the whole class.

I'm inviting everyone, she says, reading my mind. *The whole eighth grade graduating class.*

It's in three weeks, Saturday, noon.

She sends the date.

It wouldn't be the same without you.

Okay, I'll try to make it, I type.

And then she says that she has to go because her kid needs her, but we should talk again soon.

I stare at the blinker for a few minutes, my hands hovering over the keys but typing nothing, just letting my mind wander. It would be nice to see everyone.

My middle school years were quite formative and I had close friends. I lived there for three whole years, and sometimes I feel like I grew up there more than I ever did in high school.

I went to three different elementary schools, one middle school, and two high schools and pretty much gave up on making friends. It's not that I wasn't friendly, it was more that I didn't want to have any long-term connections because I would just have to move again and it was too painful.

While Dad subjected me to all of the moving until I was eighteen, I did it myself in college. I went to California State University, Long Beach for a year, then moved to Illinois after getting into University of Chicago. I didn't like that. I moved back to attend University of Southern California. I graduated from there with a degree in psychology, probably because my whole life, I tried to figure out why people did the things they did.

It didn't really matter what my major was unless I was going into engineering or pre-med, or something like that. I figured law enforcement would be something that would work for me, and all I needed was a degree.

For a little bit, I considered a graduate degree in psychology.

But when I said no to the FBI, my dad refused to cosign any more loans. So, I went to the LAPD recruitment fair on a whim.

I needed a job. I had a lot of student loans to pay back. The fact that my particular law enforcement agency choice also aggravated my dad was just the cherry on top.

41

CHARLOTTE

Just as I turn my attention to start working on a report, I glance over at Will sitting at his desk a little bit across the way.

We haven't talked much since our argument at the park, uncertain as to how to proceed or what to do.

Well, that's not true.

I know exactly what I need to do, but whether I'm willing to do it is a whole other story. He didn't ask me one way or another, and I appreciate that. In fact, he tried to protect me.

Much to my own disappointment, I did not listen. I did not take his advice. I should have, I know that much.

I was an idiot not to. I would have plausible deniability, but of course, I don't.

Now that I know everything that he's up to, what decisions I make about telling the Lieutenant and Internal Affairs, that's on me. And the more time that passes, the more complicit I become, and yet inaction is a difficult thing to turn away from.

What if no one finds out?

What if we can just keep the secret like I kept that other one?

A rush of cold sweat runs down my back. I can feel the inside of my shirt sticking to my bare skin.

No, this secret is nothing like the other one. It's completely different. It's improper and career-ending perhaps, but it's not so devastating like the other one. The mere thought of conflating the two makes me sick to my stomach.

When Will and I exchange glances, he doesn't wink or give me a forced smile. He doesn't say thank you for keeping it a secret. He just looks at me in that knowing way of someone who understands something deep about me, the way a very close friend would in a difficult time. There's no manipulation of emotions. There's just the authenticity of simply seeing me, and for now it's enough.

"Pierce, Torch," Lieutenant Soderstrom's loud voice booms around the poorly insulated walls.

This place needs some carpeting, at least a rug, because the squeaking of the linoleum floor grates on my existence. No one else seems to notice the constant buzz of the voices echoing around the walls, the loudness of it all like a poorly designed restaurant. The sound acoustics give me a headache. I thought of mentioning it to someone, but who?

Lieutenant Soderstrom has the body of someone who played football in college and high school. Cal State San Bernardino, in fact, a proud graduate. But he never stopped eating like a football player. He's well built with big broad shoulders, strong, and a belly to match.

He has a thick neck and broad shoulders, wide set eyes and a thick head of hair, tan skin. Sometimes he makes crude and inappropriate jokes, but he means well, so we let it pass.

He's in his mid-50s, married with two kids in high school. He laughs with a big booming voice, and he has always been a good boss. I don't say that lightly because I've met plenty of bad ones.

"When are you guys going to bring in Erin Lowry for an official sit down?" he asks.

"Soon," I say, clearing my throat.

"Okay, good. She has a lot to explain."

"I'm still waiting on the toxicology report," I say. "Just to know for sure about her state of mind."

"Yeah," he says, clicking his mouth.

It’s not so much a nervous habit, but just an annoying one that he never seems to notice. He used to carry a toothpick around until someone told him that it's not exactly polite. So now he makes this clicking sound with the left side of his face, like a smirk almost.

"We need to talk to her, bring her in."

"She lawyered up," Will says. “Christopher Flynn."

"Perfect.” Lieutenant rolls his eyes.

Christopher's reputation precedes him. We've dealt with him on a few occasions, and each time he got his clients off, the ones that we were certain were guilty for sure.

“So, what do we think?”

“What do you mean?” I ask the lieutenant. "You think she did it?"

Will and I exchange glances.

"She definitely looks guilty,” I start. "She was the one who was at the scene, made the call. She has no memory of what happened. There was gun powder residue on her hands."

"But?" Lieutenant asks. "I hear a *but* coming."

"I don't know."

"She hired Christopher," Lieutenant says.

"Yeah, she did. But I mean, isn't it the case that if you hire Johnnie Cochran and you're OJ Simpson, you probably did it?"

I shrug. "Yeah, maybe in that case, but I don't know. I don't know about Erin."

"What do *you* think?" Lieutenant turns his attention to Will. "You have to think she's guilty."

"The evidence is piling up," he admits, "but I have my doubts as well."

"I think the toxicology report's going to tell us a lot," I interrupt. "If she has something in her system, she's drugged."

"You know that gunshot residue tests are not that reliable," Will adds. "They could have all sorts of eventualities and possibilities as to how it got there. We don't have any fingerprints of her handling the gun."

"Seems like she doesn't need her lawyer after all when she's got two cops who are supposed to be investigating this case, arguing for her innocence."

"We're just trying to cover all the bases," Will says.

"Well, this is where you bring her in and you try to make her talk," Lieutenant says. "You two are good at that. Not just good cop, bad cop, but also understanding cop, dickhead cop. You can switch roles, play your little game. But I want a confession."

"There are no guarantees of that," Will says.

"Of course not, but with a fabulous duo like you two, of course you can make her talk. Right? I wouldn't expect anything less."

We exchange looks.

"Come on now, kids. Who are we kidding here? She was stalking him online. She was pissed off about the baby. She snapped. Maybe she got blackout drunk before she did it, maybe not. But who else could have done it? You know it's her, I know it's her, go gather some evidence and prove it. I expect to see the interview room booked."

I open my mouth to say something else, but he shuts me down.

"I don't know if her attorney will be available today," Will says, clearing his throat.

"I want it on the schedule, Torch," Lieutenant Soderstrom snaps. "Prosecutor's breathing down my neck, this is a big case."

42

ERIN

I know that I'm not supposed to be here, but I follow her anyway. I make sure that no one is following me. I keep an eye out, looking over my shoulder just to make sure.

I can't have the police finding out that I'm anywhere near her.

Why am I here? I have to find out the truth.

Christopher is right. They're closing in on Will, and I need to do something about it. I have to find out who really did this.

I have to find out who the responsible party really is.

I also follow her for my own curiosity. Did she have anything to do with their murders? Perhaps.

But there's also so much more to Maura Foley that I need to know.

She drives a Honda CRV and she drives fast. She accelerates through yellow lights and I see her phone flickering in between the seats as she uses it to talk and gesture wildly.

There's that saying about, tell me who your friends are and I'll show you who you are. But what about girlfriends and wives? The three women that I know of (me, Susannah, Maura) we could not be more different.

Susannah was a tall, elegant dance teacher who seemed to be the kind of woman who would be offended by a four letter word, even in today's day and age. Tiffany's jewelry seemed to be made just for her as well as the Vera Wang gown and wedding with a $50,000 price tag.

Maura, on the other hand, seems different. She's shorter than I am, a little plumper. There's an edginess to her that neither I nor Susannah possess. While I'm an attorney by trade who quit working to stay home with the children that we never had, where does Maura fit in? Is she the first love that never got away? Technically she was the one that Derek had lied to the most.

As I follow her, keeping a few cars in between us at all times, she surprises me. Instead of running errands with the usual stops at Target, Costco, and perhaps Trader Joe's, Maura pulls into 24 Hour Fitness. The child is not with her. She leaves her car in the parking lot and disappears through the double doors.

What do I do now, I wonder?

I glance down at my clothes, leggings, casual sweatshirt.

I look like I belong here.

Maybe if I walk in, I can find her… and what?

My mind goes blank.

I didn't want to confront her, just find out more about who she is.

I look at the time. It has been a few minutes, and without giving it any more thought, I just get out, walk through the double doors, nod to the woman at the front desk, and head straight to the women's locker room, following the group of women scanning their cards. I pretend to do the same but instead slip in behind the last one.

The woman at the front desk doesn't notice and I disappear behind the big W sign.

It's early morning, barely eight o'clock, and the place is filled with moms who have recently dropped off their kids. This isn't the hardcore 5:00 a.m. CrossFit crowd. This is the casual, let's do a yoga class, stay in shape, kind of audience.

The locker room doors are made to look like wood, upscale, and there are benches in front of each row. I walk along the aisles searching for Maura. Perhaps she just went straight to the class, or maybe straight to the weight room. I walk past the last part with the showers. I don't pull back any curtains. Instead, I head toward the exit.

I probably missed her. Maybe talking to her in the weight room or on the treadmill will be better. It's a more public place after all.

But then the door of the bathroom swings open and she comes out.

MAURA RECOGNIZES ME IMMEDIATELY. She glares, shaking her head.

"You killed Derek," she snaps, throwing her finger in my face.

Curls escape the hair band at the nape of her neck.

"What are you doing here?" Maura snaps.

I thought I would have the upper hand. I'd be the one calling the shots, but I'm not. I'm somehow caught off guard.

Her big wide eyes narrow and flicker.

"I'm here to talk to you." I say, clearing my head.

Focus, Erin, you can do this.

You're here to get answers.

You deserve them.

"I did nothing wrong," I say, clearing my throat, looking directly at her. "Derek and I were married for years. I thought we were in love. I took his last name. I thought we were making a life together."

"Do you want a present for that or what?"

"At least some sort of acknowledgement," I add. "He was my husband, but apparently he was married to you all of this time."

"Yes, he was," Maura says.

"Did you know about me?"

"No, absolutely not," she snaps.

Dressed in an oversized sweater that's falling off one shoulder, high waisted leggings, and high tops, she looks like the epitome of cool, but also like someone from an eighties music video.

"I knew nothing about you," Maura says. "Or Susannah, until the police told me."

She leans against the wall, her arms folded into herself and I see that the outwardly arrogant self-assured woman is something of a facade.

The person standing before me, fragile and broken, is who she really is. She's hurt, just like I am.

"Can you tell me what's going on, Maura?" I ask.

"I want to ask you the same thing. How could you think that Derek was married to you all this time when he and I were together?"

She looks up at me, tilting her head to one side, her hair clearly dirty and out of place, falling in her face. She came here to work out. I've looked like this much of a wreck for days for no reason whatsoever.

"I guess I'm asking you this," I say, "because it's the same question I've had and ask myself over and over again for this whole time. I mean, how could this have happened? Were there no signs at all?"

"He told me he was working a lot, traveling."

"That's what he told me, too," I say. "So, were you together when we were in Pennsylvania?"

She nods.

"My father was sick and I had to stay here and take care of him. He went there to law school because Penn was as good as it gets. We stayed in touch over the phone. We talked a lot and then afterward he got a job here and I was so happy. He was coming home. Everyone told me that I shouldn't get my hopes up, but I knew that Derek really loved me."

"When did you get married?" I ask.

"Right before he started law school. It was stupid, I guess, but I thought it would keep us together."

"So you were married the whole time that I knew him?"

Maura nods.

A big knot forms in the back of my throat. I feel like a fool, an idiot, something of a common occurrence now.

I ask her more questions and find out he had lied to her for a lot longer than he had lied to me. He was married when we started dating, but his wife lived across the country and couldn't visit often because of financial circumstances. The few times she came out were the same dates that he had to go home.

It didn't happen often until we moved out to California. That was when he really started working away a lot. He supposedly had cases in Seattle, Denver, San Francisco, all over the west coast.

"So, every time that he said he was traveling, he was with me," Maura says. "We went on trips and had family time."

"And where did you live?"

"The house you visited. It's quite close to my parents. You can get a lot of space in Desert Rocks for that price. And that was fine by me."

I search my mind for all the inconsistencies. Derek did travel a lot, but he couldn't have gone to see his wife *every* time, right?

"You look shell shocked," Maura says.

"How are you not?”

“Once I found out about you, I just knew that he was such a liar. He cheated on me in college, but I thought we got over it. I forgave him. It's one of the reasons we got married. I thought that would make him mine forever. What a joke.”

When she laughs and her oversized sweatshirt falls off her shoulder further, she pushes it back up.

“So, when I found out about Susannah, it was, I don't know…absurd. I couldn't help but laugh rather than cry. I guess you're not experiencing the same humor."

I shake my head no. I look past her at my face in the mirror.

Lips turned down.

Bags under my eyes.

Sallow skin.

"I just can't believe that he did that, that this was my life,” I say, pushing my hair up to give it a little bit more volume and realizing just how greasy it is.

"You'll get used to it, I guess,” Maura says with a casual smile. "I'm sorry. I don't mean to be insensitive. I just have a whole lot of my own drama to deal with. And I can't really hold your hand through this."

"I don't expect you to."

"Good."

"So what about his murder?" I ask.

She crosses her arms and leans back, something of another part of her is back. That confidence, that wittiness.

"I thought you'd tell me about it," Maura says.

"Tell you about what?"

"About how you killed them because you're so angry and upset."

"No, I had nothing to do with that," I say. "Of course I didn't kill them."

"If *you* didn't kill them and *I* didn't kill them, then *who* killed them?"

I shrug. She coughs. Her voice is a few octaves lower now. She walks past me toward the sink, looks at herself in the mirror, and then splashes some water on her face.

"Maura, I'm telling you I had nothing to do with their murders. I mean, I was there and I found them, but that was it."

"Okay. That's the story you want to stick with? You think the cops are going to buy it?"

"It's not up to them to buy it. It's the truth."

"Well, you have to *sell* it to them. You have to make sure that they actually believe you," she says.

"You know, you're not anything like I thought you would be," I say quietly after a long pause. "When we first met, you were so different when you were with your child."

That word rings almost as if there was an echo in the small bathroom, in the small sink area. But there isn't.

“She’s not Derek’s," she says.

I look at her, feeling my eyes practically bulge out of my head.

"What do you mean, she's not his?"

"Derek's not the only one who's made mistakes. We tried to have kids for a while, kind of on and off. He really didn't want them. And then it took a while for me to get pregnant. We had our share of fights. So, one day I went to a bar and met an old friend. He was kind of like that guy, dated a few of my girlfriends, but we were friendly with each other, but never romantic. We started joking around. Drank a little too much. Derek and I were a bit on the outs. I was angry. I felt like something was wrong. That was right before I found out about you. We slept together that night.”

I let out a small sigh of relief that her child isn’t Derek’s.

"I was so scared that I might be pregnant, not by my husband. But then I found out about you."

"You did? How?"

"I dropped him off at the airport, but I got lost, missed my exit. So I went around again and I saw him exit and get in the car with *you*. It was a shock but then a relief."

43

ERIN

Christopher wanted to put this off for later, but I didn't. As soon as they listed the two times that they were available, tomorrow and a week from now, I told him that it would have to be tomorrow.

I want to get this over with. Done.

I have nothing else to add and I want them to finally believe me. But when I arrive at the interrogation room, I get nervous.

The only person that seems at all interested in being here is me. Christopher and Detective Pierce and Will look like they're the ones being interrogated.

Will and I haven't talked about where we stand. If Detective Pierce knows anything, she's not talking, least of all on camera, in this room with my attorney present. I figure that I should use this to my advantage. Why not? If she has something to hide and Will is on my side, it can only be something good.

Besides, I can always hold on to this bit of information in my back pocket, just in case. That's why I don't tell Christopher, not yet.

It's not that I don't trust him. Of course, I do.

But it's a secret that I share with Will and I need to protect him so that he can protect me in this situation. At least for now.

The room has a window and a table for all of us to sit in comfortable chairs. It doesn't look so much like an interrogation room, but more like an office meeting space, a place you would interview for a job.

After brief introductions, Detective Pierce gets right to the point. I don't know whether we're being recorded, but Christopher assumes that we are. He prepped me late last night, about everything that I should and shouldn't say. And by the fact that we're meeting today, just a day later, he seems rather uneasy about me remembering everything, but I do.

We go over my statement. I repeat everything that happened as I remember it. And when we hit the part that I don't remember, I don't make up anything.

Instead, I just say, "I already covered this and I don't have anything else to add."

"No additional memories?" Detective Pierce asks.

I shake my head. "No, unfortunately not."

When the conversation turns to the results of the gunshot residue test, Christopher does as good a job of defending me and getting them to prove their case as he did with Sandra. I offer no additional explanation.

I don't place myself anywhere that I hadn't been before, just like he had instructed. And overall, when they take a break, everything seems to be in our favor. They return with two cans of Coke and a coffee for me, which I only accept on a ceremonial premise. I don't really want it, but I don't want to say no.

"As your own evidence shows you," Christopher says. "Erin had no blood splatter on her body-"

"She had blood on her," Detective Pierce interrupts.

"From when she slipped and fell. No blood splatter that was created from drops of blood radiating from the impact of a bullet or blunt instrument."

Christopher pauses for effect.

"As I was saying, Erin had no blood splatter on her body and her prints were not on the gun. And as for motive? You have the original wife, the only one."

"You're telling me that Erin was not scorned?" Detective Pierce asks, raising an eyebrow.

Dressed in flats and a black suit jacket to match, she looks like the epitome of a television cop, especially with the badge and the gun on her hip.

"I wouldn't say that, Erin was upset," Christopher admits. “It was definitely a big shock to her to find out that the man who she thought she was married to was cheating on her. And that's why she made all of those posts and calls to the cell phone, even after he got remarried. But she wasn't the only one that he had lied to, was she, Detective Pierce? What about Maura Foley?"

"Maura has an alibi,” Will says. My eyes flick up at him, but he avoids them and stays neutral.

"I'm not sure what kind of an alibi Maura has, but you better check it again. She was his first and only wife. She was the one who had to uncover the humiliation of not knowing that her husband was cheating on her, engaged in very long-term, committed relationships with two other women. You don't think that made her mad?"

"I'm sure it did," Detective Pierce says. "But she wasn't the one stalking him."

"Exactly, that's my point,” Christopher says, sitting back in his chair, reclining slightly, tossing his leg up and crossing it at the knee.

"Maura was making plans. She was trying to frame Erin because she knew that she wasn't handling the breakup very well."

"I find that hard to believe," Detective Pierce says.

"Why is that?" Christopher pushes.

"Maura has a very strong alibi. She wasn't found at the scene of the crime."

"And that is?"

"She was attending her father's funeral. It was earlier that day."

A silence falls over the room.

"Surely, the funeral wasn't at night?" Christopher points out.

"No, of course not. But she was staying at her sister's house. And they had a house full of people."

"Who were tracking all of her movements at night? They weren't sleeping?"

"There are cameras set up," Detective Pierce says, "on the property and they were running. We checked the footage. She was there, she didn't leave. Her car was there."

Christopher shrugs.

"Well, I guess then you have your job all cut out for you. You have to go find the perpetrator who did this, who wasn't my client."

"No, I don't think so," Will says. "I think that our job is actually quite easy. We had to look at the evidence and figure out who could have done this. Who would've had the means, opportunity, motive, all that jazz, and there's really only one person. Your client."

Cold sweat runs down my back. Is he really doing me like this?

Does he really believe this?

I look over at Detective Pierce. It's her fault, she's the one who's convinced him of this. Then I look closer at him.

He doesn't give me a wink or a smile, nothing that obvious, but there's something in his demeanor that tells me, that he is putting on a show.

Something is different here. This isn't meant for me to hear, I'm just a bystander.

I hold onto that hope. It might be something of a delusion. It might not be true at all, but what else do I have?

We talk more. Will and Detective Pierce asking the same questions in different ways. When they try to go over everything for the third time, Christopher cuts them off.

“We’re done here,” he says.

“We still have a lot to talk about,” Will says.

"We did you the courtesy," he says. "We met with you, went over everything, made more statements. Now, we're going to go."

"We're not finished,” Detective Pierce says.

“Yes, we are. So unless you're going to arrest my client right now and detain her, we're going to be on our way."

My throat closes up as I wait for their answer.

44

WILL

"What was that?" Lieutenant Soderstrom says as soon as we get back to the conference room with everyone watching the interrogation.

Charlotte has braced herself for impact, but I let myself go for a moment, thinking that it sounded like we did a good job. The lieutenant isn't happy, however. Pissed is more like it.

"You should have pushed her more on the Maura angle."

"How?" Charlotte asks. "What would you have us do? She had her scum attorney in there representing her interests. You know how it is, you know how good he is."

Christopher lets his clients talk just enough to give us nothing and to toy with us. He's not one of those lawyers that clams up. He's certain that every single dirtbag that he represents is innocent until proven otherwise.

"You two should have put more pressure on her," Lieutenant Soderstrom says. "But the truth is that I'm not really sure *you* think she did it."

"Do *you* really think that she did?" I ask. He glares at me.

Chain of command is very important in our line of work. It's what keeps everything going round in circles. Without it, everyone would be able to do what they want, and that's not exactly a good decision. Lower ranked deputies don't have as much information about what's going on. Or experience.

Lieutenant Soderstrom is our boss but watching him interact with the Assistant District Attorney Kathleen Detoro, who will be prosecuting this case, I lose a little respect for him. He's just eager to close this case. It has been all over the news, double murder of a well-known attorney. Pregnant wife, beautiful, successful young couple, and a scorned ex-wife finds out the truth about him. The press is having a field day, and we all know it. And yet, the case is impossible to close.

"I'm not trying to defend her. Don't misunderstand me," I say, appealing to both the Lieutenant and Kathleen. "The only blood that Erin had on her was from where she slipped and fell and her prints weren't anywhere on the gun. Yes, she was a scorned ex-wife who left a lot of threatening messages. And yes, she found out that they weren't even married, which is of course terrible."

Lieutenant Soderstrom and Kathleen exchange looks. She pinches the manila folder in between her fingertips a little harder.

"Maura, the real ex-wife has a pretty much ironclad alibi, unless we find something that disproves it. But it doesn't mean that we can railroad Erin into being the one who did this."

"There's a toxicology report that just came in," Charlotte adds. "We didn't bring it up in the interrogation to buy some time. But of course we'll have to reveal this to her attorney, and it's going to be the nail in the coffin of our case in a bad way."

"What did they find?" Lieutenant asks.

"Erin had a date rape drug, GHB, in her bloodstream," I say. "This clears her and explains why she had no memory of what had happened leading up to her walking around the house. Someone had drugged her. But who?"

"She could have taken it recreationally," Kathleen points out.

I nod. "It's a possibility."

"She has been drinking a lot," she adds.

"That's going to be hard to prove in court," Charlotte says.

“Are you telling me how to do my job?” Kathleen furrows her brows, pulling her arms across her chest.

“I'm just stating the facts of the case,” Charlotte says. “This amount of GHB... I don't know. Yes, perhaps she did take recreationally, but she has absolutely no history of drug use. I don't even know where she could have gotten it from.”

“I thought that you two knew her quite well and all of her movements.”

"I've been following her around," I say. “Yes, I've been investigating her.”

“And you really think that she didn't do it?” Lieutenant Soderstrom asks.

“If she were found with the murder weapon, blood splatter that was clearly from a gunshot, then maybe yes. But the gunshot residue? Her lawyer's right, and you know it. It can show up just being in the vicinity. Whoever drugged her probably discharged a weapon where she was passed out. And if she drugged herself for recreational purposes, then when would she have fired the gun? When would she have committed the murders? It just seems very unlikely. She looks guilty, but the evidence doesn't line up.”

"As you know, GHB stays in the system for about eight hours," Charlotte adds. “We don't know how long she’d been out, but perhaps finding out where she got it or who gave it to her. Where she got it if she was the one who took it and bought it, or who gave it to her and who drugged her would be the key to us solving this crime, this case. The problem is that we're too early. We don't have enough information. And with an attorney like that, we're not going to catch her for a while if it was her."

This conversation seems to leave the lieutenant and the ADA more than mildly annoyed, but it's the way it goes sometimes.

I stand by everything I've said.

A FEW HOURS LATER, I get a call from the ADA. She tells me that she was forced to tell Christopher the results of the toxicology report, it being part of the discovery and all.

"I'm not happy about it, as you can imagine," Kathleen says.

"You could have waited," I offer.

"No point. He asked specifically. He already knew that the results were in. Flynn's the kind of attorney who does his research. Dots his i's and crosses his t's. There's no point in hiding this from him. So assume that Erin Lowry knows what's going on. I'm not asking you to make a case against her. I'm asking you to solve this fricking case. It's all over the news every night, and I'm sick of it. My boss is going to lose his reelection campaign based on it if it's not solved. The public demands answers. And all the web sleuths out there on all of those forums and Facebook groups, they're saying that it's her. Clearly they don't have all the evidence, but it's making it harder and harder for me to make a case."

"What do you want me to do?" I ask.

“I want you to investigate everyone connected to Derek and Susannah, but specially Derek. If it's not the two ex-wives, then I'm sure he had lots of other enemies. He was a lawyer, after all.”

“He did represent lots of bad guys,” I admit.

“Any of them make any threats?”

“Yes. We investigated a couple that did. Well, there are probably others who hold grudges who didn't. If it's not a personal angle when it comes to his romantic life, it's something he would have done in his private life. His wife wouldn't end up dead otherwise.”

“We really need an arrest here,” Kathleen says. “We need to show the public that this is going somewhere. Do you understand?”

I nod, feeling her desperation.

“We're talking about our careers here,” she adds.

“You're telling me you want me to arrest anyone?” I ask.

"No, of course not," she says, being defensive. "I want you to do your job, which I think you've been kind of neglecting."

"I've been doing no such thing," I snap. "You see the evidence. You know what we're dealing with. I'm not in the business of arresting innocent people and framing people for crimes they didn't commit. If that's what you want from a cop, you go to someone else."

When I hang up the phone, I stare at it for a few minutes. If only she knew how involved I really am in this case.

45

ERIN

I pull into the school's parking lot twenty minutes before the bell rings, because I know that she'll be there doing paperwork. Sandra hates waiting in line at pickup so she gets there early to get a good spot and her kids are told to be the first ones out of school. Outside of the teachers' cars, she's the only one there right before the place becomes a zoo.

I watch her for a few minutes with her big legal pad and her paperwork set up on a specifically designed table that attaches to the steering wheel. That's how devoted she is to never missing any work, or at least utilizing all of her free time in the most efficient manner possible.

I knock on the window of her white Mercedes and watch her head whip around startled. I raise my hand up to tell her and say, "I'm sorry," even though I doubt that she can hear me through the glass. She rolls down the window just as I grab the door handle, which doesn't open.

"Can I talk to you?" I ask.

When Sandra unlocks it, I get in. Moving some of her paperwork, she folds her hands neatly across the tray pretending to be a desk. She turns her body slightly in my direction.

"I'm here to apologize," I say. "I shouldn't have said any of those things. I mean, I was angry."

"I would never give you a subpar defense," Sandra says. "I take my job very seriously."

"Yes, I know. I know." I nod.

"I was just angry with myself more than anyone else for being in that whole situation and we're friends and I don't want to lose that. You're really important to me."

She looks down at her long manicured fingers. The nails are cut short, professional, a nude color, inoffensive to clients. Professionalism is the reason why she spends so much money on straightening her coarse, 4C textured hair.

She has always done it without any complaints except once when we had a few too many drinks. Sandra told me how much she had wished that she could just let her hair go natural, be one of those women who embraces her afro.

But she's afraid that her clients would think less of her as an attorney and she wouldn't get as far in the law firm.

"It's hard enough to be a woman in this line of work," she said. "I can't really draw too much attention to my race as well."

Today her hair is silky straight. Her lipstick gives her a nice pink sheen and everything about her is put together in the way that people expect from their attorneys handling paperwork.

No personality. Lots of competence.

"Are we friends again?" I ask after a long pause. "I'm really sorry about what I said. It was stupid. I know that you're really good at your job, and I'm sorry that I hired your nemesis instead."

"From what I hear, he's doing quite a good job for you."

"Oh, yeah? Are you checking up on the case?"

"Of course. You were my client and a friend and I'm worried about you."

"Well, good news. Toxicology came back that I had GHB in my system."

"Date rape drug?" Sandra asks. "And that's what you call good news?"

"You know what I mean. It's not good news, but good news for the case. Clearly, I wasn't someone who would ever drug herself. Someone must have drugged me, and that's how I ended up there."

"But who?" Sandra asks.

I shrug. "Your guess is as good as mine."

"Do you have any enemies you're not telling me about?" Sandra asks, leaning forward, only half joking.

That accusatory tone in her voice makes me feel a little uneasy.

"You know as much as I do," I say, biting my lower lip.

"Listen, I have to run into the school to go to the bathroom before the girls come out and this whole parking lot just becomes a mess of traffic. Would you mind waiting here? The girls would love to see you. We can grab some pizza, just hang out."

"Yeah, that would be great," I say.

I sit in her car for a few minutes, staring out into space, thinking of nothing in particular. I didn't have to come here, but it feels like it was the right thing to do.

I miss her as a friend, and maybe it wasn't a great idea to hire her as an attorney. I don't know how ferocious she would've been against the police or if they had taken her as seriously as they've taken Christopher Flynn, but all that's in the past. I'm glad that we can get over this and resume the friendship.

As I reach into my purse to put on some lip gloss, I hear the loud vibrating sound of a phone against a hard surface. I have mine on silent, and so I look around and open the little compartment in between the two seats. That's where I see it in the middle of getting charged.

It's a phone call from Shawn Nieves.

I let it go to voice mail and a few minutes later, I hear a beep. As I try to get the compartment closed back up, pushing it in and trying to pull at it all without much success, the screen flickers and the message shows up.

Grayson still owes Derek $50k from before. He never paid. I checked the bank records.

I stare at the text until it disappears.

"Grayson, Grayson. Who's Grayson?" I say to myself.

Thomas Grayson? He's that guy who was a client of Derek's, but Shawn investigated him, said that he had an ironclad alibi.

He was on a flight to Vegas.

"50K in debt. What's that about?" I wonder.

A minute later, Sandra gets in the car, her girls in tow. I'm about to get out so that we can exchange hugs, but she tells me to stay put.

“We've got to get out of here before we get stuck for an hour," she says. "Put on your seat belts."

"Mom is crazy about avoiding traffic," one says.

"It honestly makes her more anxious than any cars can.” The other laughs.

I try to put Shawn's text out of my mind, but I can't think of anything else.

I have to wait to talk to her when we have some privacy and when the pizza slices run out and the girls bury their heads in their phones while doing homework around the coffee table, I pull Sandra aside.

"Listen, when you weren't in the car, your phone went off and it was Shawn, but I let it go to voice mail."

She nods, looking unconcerned.

"But then the text came and it just popped up on the screen."

"Okay, what are you saying, Erin?"

"Did you see what he wrote?"

She shakes her head no, pulling out her phone. She reads it and then looks up at me.

"That's Thomas Grayson," she says.

"Yeah, I know. He owes Derek fifty grand."

"Yes, I guess so." She shrugs.

"Isn't that a big deal?"

"Shawn seems to think so."

"And you don't?"

"I don't know. I just found out about this, Erin. Let me think."

She taps her nails on the quartz countertops.

"Yeah, it's definitely a big deal," she agrees.

I force a smile. "What does this mean?"

"I'm not sure. I mean, you know as much as I do. He was one of Derek's main clients. I'm not exactly sure what kind of work they did together. Attorney-client privilege and all that."

"What kind of business is Grayson in? Real estate?"

"A lot of real estate, commercial mainly. Owns a lot of buildings around town. But I assume he took care of some work for him that involved purchases, that kind of thing. Who knows, really? By the time I left, Derek and Christopher were getting in bed with a lot of shady people."

"What do you mean by that?"

"Drug dealers, laundering money."

"What?" I ask.

"I didn't want to tell you. Maybe I shouldn't have. I don't know. I can't be specific about it. Attorney-client privilege, and you know that I take that seriously. But they were taking on a lot of clients that were just not making the firm look good. I mean, I know they worked on a lot of murder cases."

"Yes?"

"But there are murder cases and then there are *murder* cases where they're executions by the cartels."

"What?" I ask, my mouth dropping. "Is that what Thomas Grayson was involved in?"

"Thomas Grayson was Mr. Moneybags. His firm built hotels around town. He made an impact on the economy. He wasn't in trouble with any criminal issues, and I don't know exactly why they were working together."

"But if he had all that money, why would he care about $50,000? I mean, why wouldn't he just pay up?"

"I don't know. I don't know if that's significant or not. You know as much as I do. That's what Shawn wrote."

I nod, biting my lower lip.

"I guess the good thing is that the police aren't after me anymore," I say after a long pause.

"Yeah." Sandra nods. "But somebody else is after you, whoever put that GHB in your system and framed you for Derek and Susannah's murders."

46

ERIN

I get up extra early to make sure that I have enough time. I got my outfit ready the day before. It's laying out on the chair next to my bed.

Pencil skirt, comfortable top, a dress suit jacket to match, and black pumps with a small heel. Sexy and professional, but comfortable. I splurged extra on these since I've never been a huge fan of heels.

I look at myself in the mirror.

Others may dress a little bit more flashy for the first day of work, but I want to fit in. I don't want to draw any attention. I don't want anyone asking where I've been all this time, even though I know everyone will.

Sandra encouraged me to go back to work, but she didn't exactly offer me a position. Only Christopher did. And, after everything that he has done for me, I'm more than grateful.

The case is still, of course, unsolved and I steady myself for the rumor mill that's about to begin. I wonder how many associates know that I'm coming back to work and I just hope that there is plenty of new blood to help me blend into the background.

After a breakfast of some avocado toast and a cup of dark coffee, just to get me energized for the day, I grab my bag and head out. But just as I open the garage door, I see him standing in my driveway. Shawn Nieves.

I look at him twice in the rearview mirror. He takes a few steps forward and comes around to the driver's side.

"I need to talk to you," he says. "It's urgent."

"It's my first day of work. I can't be late."

"It's very important. Your life is in danger," Shawn says and swallows deeply.

I stare at him.

"Thomas Grayson," he says. "He's back in town and I need to get you into hiding right now."

The name shakes me to the core.

My suspicions have been right all along. He does have something to do with this.

"Why? Why is he after me?"

"I don't know exactly," Shawn says, "but it's not a good idea for you to go to work today. I need to have you somewhere where I can protect you and we can figure everything out."

We continue to go back and forth, but the longer that we talk, the more convinced I become that Shawn is right. He's Sandra's friend. He's protected me so far and I should trust him on this.

"But what about my first day? I can't just *not* show up."

"Why don't you come with me now and we can figure all this out later? If you stay here or you go somewhere else in your car, I won't be able to protect you," Shawn says. "I got a motel room, a nondescript place where they'll really have to look for you to find you. Come, we can figure this out."

I take a deep breath and give him a slight nod. Grabbing my purse out of the car, along with my phone and water bottle, I follow him to his Kia, a nondescript kind of vehicle like so many on the road.

I tell him about the text message that I found on Sandra's phone yesterday and he nods with understanding.

We talk about it for a little while, same things that we discussed with Sandra. When we get to the Motel 6 on the side of the highway bordering a tall mountain to one side and a Pinky's on the other, I ask, "So you knew about this yesterday?"

"Yes. Well, I had my suspicions, but I wasn't sure. I've been looking more into him trying to figure out who did this to you. The toxicology report didn't exactly come back with good news, did it?"

"Well, it cleared my name, I guess," I say.

"Yeah, but it seems like Grayson is the likeliest suspect. Or someone working for him."

"But I have no idea who he is. Why is he framing me?"

"He could have done something to Derek himself. Derek was his attorney, who knows what their relationship was really like and what Derek knew. But then he needed a fall guy. You."

"Me?" I say, gasping.

We make our way to the room. He already checked in. It's on the second floor, the door heading straight out onto the landing. He flips on the light by the dining room and it swings from side to side from his pulling on the string.

I sit on the edge of one of the double beds with my purse next to me, trying to process everything.

When Shawn goes to use the bathroom, I reach for my phone and call Christopher. He doesn't answer so I text.

I can't come into work today.

Shawn is here and we're at a motel. Apparently my life is in danger over this guy, Thomas Grayson, who's probably the one who killed Derek.

I'm so sorry I'm late.

I'm so sorry that I won't be there.

"What are you doing?" Shawn asks, grabbing the phone away from me just as I click send.

"I needed to tell Christopher why I didn't show up."

"No one is supposed to know that we're here."

"He's my attorney for Christ's sake."

"What did I tell you?" Shawn asks. "No one is supposed to know that we're here. That's how you're going to remain safe. You hungry? I can get some food from Pinky's."

"No, I'm fine. I just ate," I say, staring at the ancient television before me.

"Can I have my phone back?" I say after a few moments.

"Only if you promise not to contact anyone."

"Okay, I promise," I say.

Hours pass slowly when you have nothing to do and a lot to worry about. I play a few games of Dots on my phone, a simple app where the goal is to connect three or four dots in a row and find specific patterns.

It's mindless, but it passes the time.

Shawn flips around to different channels then watches something on his phone, luckily, with earphones so I don't have to hear.

Finally, it's noon.

It's been long enough that my stomach starts to grumble and he offers to go to Pinky's, the pink and turquoise 1950s themed diner across the street, for some takeout. Shawn texts me the menu and I pick a milkshake and curly fries as well as a vegetarian bean burger with avocado dressing.

I doubt that they served that in the fifties, but it sounds good and my mouth waters when I see the picture on the menu.

While he's gone, I look at Christopher's text back to me.

Where are you? Are you okay?

Yes, I'm fine, I text back and then decide to place a call.

"What's going on?" Christopher sounds frantic.

I tell him what happened this morning, summing it up in as few words as possible.

"He just showed up here and said my life was in danger. I'm not sure what to do, but we're just hiding out."

"Do you really think this is what's happening?"

"I don't know, probably. Shawn has always been good at finding out the truth, hasn't he?"

I nod. "I was thinking of reaching out to Sandra and telling her-"

"No," Christopher cuts me off. "Absolutely not."

"Look, I know that you two have your differences, but she's my friend."

"The fewer people that know about this, the better," Christopher says. "You just don't know who to trust."

"Of course I can trust Sandra. She's the one who told me about Grayson in the first place."

"What exactly did she tell you?" Christopher asks.

"That Derek was working for him at the firm, that he was shady. What can you tell me about that?"

"Nothing. I had very little interaction with Grayson myself. But yes, Derek did work for him, but everything is attorney-client privilege, as you know. So the few times that I saw him in the hallways, we just exchanged pleasantries and that's it."

"Do you think he's dangerous?" I ask.

"What's the story here?" Christopher asks. "That Grayson was the one that killed Derek and Susannah and is, what, framing you?"

"Yeah, possibly."

"For $50,000?" Christopher asks. "That he can pay back."

"Yeah, I know it sounds stupid, but there could be something else."

At that moment, Shawn walks through the door and I hang up the phone.

"What are you doing?" he asks.

"I'm sorry."

"Who were you talking to?" He puts the food wrapped in white plastic bags on the dining room table.

I had opened the curtains to have some light in this hole of a motel room, but he quickly closes them.

"I told you that your life is in danger and you're making calls talking to your lawyer?"

"Yes. I'm talking to my lawyer. What's the big deal?" I say. "This isn't quite adding up."

"What's not adding up?" Shawn asks.

"Why is Grayson framing me? And how do you know that my life is even in danger?"

Shawn sits down.

"I know because I'm trailing him," he says. "I've been following him for a while. He's been my primary suspect in this whole situation. Sandra hired me to protect you, so that's what I've been doing."

"What exactly have you been doing?" I ask. "You can't keep any more secrets from me, Shawn. Things aren't adding up and I need you to explain."

"Okay," he says, opening his Styrofoam container and grabbing a plastic fork. "Ask me anything."

"What did you find out? Why did you text that to Sandra?"

"I found out that one of the clients, Thomas Grayson, didn't pay Derek the $50,000 that he owed. I do not know why. I suspect that this debt has something to do with Derek's death."

I think about it for a moment. I sit down across from him, opening and taking a sip of my thick milkshake, chocolaty with just enough sweetness and a cherry on top. I haven't had a milkshake in years and I indulge and greedily take a few gulps.

"But that doesn't really make sense," I say.

"What doesn't make sense?" Shawn sucks down some Sprite, making a loud sucking sound.

"Why would he do that? Grayson has money, right? I mean, he's got a lot of hotels. $50,000 seems like a lot of money for an average person, but not for someone like that."

"Perhaps, but rich people have a tendency to continue pretending to be rich long after they are no longer as wealthy," Shawn says, biting into his burger.

"Okay, so possibly," I agree, opening the top of my milkshake and spooning some of it into my mouth. "But what about Susannah? If it was Derek that he owed this debt to and didn't want to pay, why kill Susannah and the baby?"

"Maybe she got in the way," Shawn says. "Maybe she was there and she wasn't supposed to be. Who knows. She was probably just a casualty of war the way that so many others are."

We finish our food, going back and forth. I ask questions, he offers possible explanations.

"The thing is that I don't know what's going on any more than you do."

"Well, that's not true," Shawn scoffs.

"What are you talking about?"

"Did Derek ever mention a file?" Shawn asks.

"A file? What kind of file?"

"I don't know exactly. I don't know what's on it, but I saw in a couple of Grayson's emails that he was looking for a file that Derek had."

"You have access to Grayson's emails?"

"I use a program to break in. Thought maybe I could get some info about what he's up to. And that's when I saw the threats against you that someone had put out and that he wanted you dead."

"What?" I ask.

"I didn't want to go and tell you all of this to protect you, but clearly you're just not one to listen to reason."

"Yes, I would like answers to what's going on with my life," I say. "I'm sorry about that."

"I'm just joking," he says. "Calm down."

"You expect me to be calm? You're telling me all these things and that someone put out a hit on me and wants me dead. There's a file I have no idea what you're talking about."

"He's looking for a USB. It's a USB. Small, the kind that fits into a computer, you know what I'm talking about? It holds data."

"Yes, of course. I'm not an idiot."

"I don't know what's on it, but he's certain that you have it. Do you?"

"No."

"Did Derek mail you something? Put something in your house?"

"I have no idea. I mean, he clearly never mailed me anything, but putting something in my house, I don't know."

"Would you mind if we go and check?"

"Check my house for a USB drive?" I ask.

He nods.

"I don't know what's on it," Shawn shrugs, "but Grayson wants it and this might be your way out of this situation."

47

WILL

Erin and I have a meeting planned at noon for which she doesn't show up. I call her a few times, hearing nothing. The calls go straight to voice mail, and text messages go unanswered as well.

This is her first day at work and I wonder if somebody invited her out to celebrate. But it's very unlike her to not show up. I wait a couple of hours, but still hear nothing.

Perhaps I'm wrong to worry. It most likely is the case, and yet something feels off, like, what if something happened?

I swing by the law firm.

I talk to the receptionist out front, asking to see Erin Lowry. The receptionist is a pleasant, if a little bit distracted, woman in her thirties. The phone keeps going off and she apologizes profusely, lifting up her finger in the air for me to wait.

The screen behind her has the names of all the partners on the pictures, and Christopher Flynn. The picture's old, and Derek is pictured next to Christopher, smiling from ear to ear. This is the same one that appeared in Super Lawyers of America, listing them as the firm to contact if you want good representation.

This firm positions itself in opposition to the sleazy ambulance chasers who advertise on TV, suing people over slip and falls, motorcycle accidents, and mesothelioma. This firm is slick, competent, expensive. But the differences between the two are negligible.

They appear respectable, but the criminals they represent are much worse. Big corporations committing major fraud and outright corruptions, even manslaughter.

Recently, over the last couple of years, they extended into criminal defense work, representing the kind of guys who are obviously guilty but who they can get off on technicalities.

All of this is under the radar. There are plenty of clients that are legit, and the firm has become big enough to appear as if they have different divisions all working apart from one another.

"Apparently, Ms. Lowry never showed up to work," the receptionist says. "I don't have her here as someone who checked in. She was supposed to get her badge and ID, but I guess she called in sick."

"How would she do that? Would she call you?"

"Yes. It's expected that you would call the main line here and I'll make a note of it. But I don't know. Perhaps she called Mr. Flynn since they do have a history."

"Has he hired any other people like this?" I say, leaning over the counter, trying to appear friendlier and not just like some scary cop here to put pressure on her. "I mean, wouldn't you say it's a little unusual that she would go work for a firm that represented her in a possible murder defense?"

"Well, no charges were filed." Christopher's voice booms from behind me. I flinch a little and turn around.

"Hey, it's nice to see you."

We shake hands. His suit costs about $3,000 more than my outfit and he looks like he lives in it.

"So let me ask you the same thing I asked your receptionist here. Erin was supposed to start work today, right?"

"Yes. But she never showed up."

"Did she call to explain?"

"Yeah. She said that she'll have to reschedule as something came up."

"She didn't explain?"

"I'm just her employer."

"Exactly," I say. "First job after all these years. I thought she'd offer some sort of explanation."

"Well, she didn't," Christopher says. "Erin and I have a history."

"Yes, I know," I say. "Isn't it a little unusual that she wouldn't show up for her first day at work?"

He shrugs.

"Isn't it also a bit unusual that you have hired a client that you are representing?"

"*Was* representing," Christopher corrects me.

"You're no longer her attorney?"

"No, I wouldn't say that," he says with a shrug. "But you and I both know she had nothing to do with those murders."

I tilt my head.

"Besides this is where she used to work with her ex-husband. She was looking for a job. It just seemed natural."

I nod, narrowing my eyes.

"Is there anything else I can help you with, Detective Torch? Because I really have to be going now."

"You let me know if you hear from her, okay?"

"No, I don't think that's a good idea," Christopher says. "If she wants to get in touch, she'll be in touch. But I think she's a little fed up with the Palm Valley Police Department."

Back in my car, I check the AirTag that I put into her bag and the Find My iPhone app with her number.

The phone is off, untraceable, at least with these means.

I sit in the parking lot for a while, trying to decide what to do. I have already gone to Erin's house. I couldn't see inside the garage so I have no idea if her car was there. Some time passes and just as I'm about to leave, I *see* him.

Christopher exits the building and heads to his car. He doesn't look around with caution. He doesn't look like he's hiding anything.

I pick up the phone and call Charlotte.

"You told me that you wanted to know what I was doing. That's the only reason I'm telling you I'm following him."

"But why?" Charlotte asks.

"Nothing about him is suspicious at all. He's not doing anything wrong," I say. "But I have to do this. I'll let you know where this goes."

48

ERIN

We get back to my house. Shawn is on a rampage, searching, asking me questions. He checks all the usual places first.

The junk drawer in the kitchen and the other one in the foyer- all the places where I tossed odd knickknacks, coins, and receipts that I meant to throw away.

"It's not here," I say. "I don't even know what you're talking about."

"You didn't get anything in the mail, anything suspicious with no return address?"

"No. No, I didn't."

"Then he must have hid it somewhere here."

"What makes you say that?" I say.

"Look, there's a very important USB drive that Derek had. It's not in his office. It's nowhere else."

"How do you even know about this?" I ask.

"It's my job to investigate, so that's what I've been doing. He must have hid it here because it wasn't at his house."

"You searched *his* house?" I ask.

Shawn's eyes flash up at me. He's checking the cupboards in the kitchen. I guess he's planning to go through the whole place.

"Look, I want you to leave," I say. "This is getting weird and I need you out of my house."

"I'm not leaving," he snaps. "This is why we're here."

"You're here to protect me, right? From this phantom threat. Well, I'm not very comfortable right now, so I need you to go."

"I don't think you're understanding this, Erin. I'm not leaving here without that USB drive."

I start to reach for my phone to call 911 but he grabs it out of my hand. Something in his demeanor shifts and all of a sudden it occurs to me that maybe he's been lying this whole time. Maybe this whole thing has just been a ruse. What if Grayson has nothing to do with this?

"If you're not going to help me find this thing, go sit over there and shut the fuck up."

Shawn opens his waistband and I see the pistol hanging out of his belt. My ears start to buzz.

What's going on?

What is happening right now? I'm unable to move, so he takes me by the shoulder and pulls me to the living room couch.

"Sit down while I look. It's here, and if it means lifting up the carpet and destroying every bit of this place, then that's what we're going to do. So it's in your best interest if you know where it is to just go ahead and tell me."

I eye the door, start to get up, but he pulls out his gun and points it at my head. "You don't want to do that. Now sit back down."

A cold sweat runs down my back. My shirt sticks to it. My heart seems to be going a million beats a minute.

But he walks around the living room, looking in every nook and cranny. Is he serious about lifting the carpet?

Whatever's on that USB drive has to be something very serious. I don't care about the house at this point. I just want out.

I glance at the door a few times while his back is turned.

The top lock is turned and I have to get that open prior to grabbing the handle.

Do I have enough time to do that if he goes to a different room? For sure.

But what if he takes me with him?

Shawn now has my phone and I'm not sure how serious he is about killing me. But then again, everything that's been happening is the complete opposite of what I thought today would be like.

"Tell me what's going on, Shawn," I say.

"You know enough," he says.

"Did Sandra even hire you?"

"Yes," he says. "Imagine the irony."

"I don't understand." I shake my head.

"You don't need to understand. You need to help me find this USB that I know that you have and then we can go our separate ways forever."

"What about Thomas Grayson?" I ask.

"What about him?" he snaps.

Shawn returns to the kitchen, just across the way. With his back turned and his body crouched down, checking the walls of the lower cabinets for anything that might be taped in there, I go for it.

I run hard toward the door, grab the top bolt, turn it to the right, and then press down on the handle below. When the door swings open, I rush out and slam straight into Christopher.

"We have to go! We can't be here! He's gone nuts!" I yell, pulling his hand to follow, but something stops me.

He grabs on too tight and his body doesn't move.

"Come on, what are you doing? Let's go."

I try to pull away but he's got an iron grip.

"Let me go! He’s coming!”

I look back for a second at Shawn and my breath gets lodged in my throat.

He's not running after me. He's not pointing the gun. He just gives a knowing nod to Christopher who pushes me back inside.

49

ERIN

My hands are bound with the long wash cloth from the kitchen, they have me tied to the coffee table. They have me sitting on the couch in the living room, my legs still free.

I can possibly still make a run for it, but there are two of them now. How far will I get? And what will happen if I flee again and don't make it?

Christopher is dressed in his exquisite suit, hair in place, shoes shined. It's almost like any other day at the office. His demeanor is also exactly the same, unfazed.

"So, that whole story about Thomas Grayson was what exactly?" I ask.

"A story," Christopher admits. "I thought it would get you to give it up but my friend here got a little impatient."

"What do you want?" I ask.

"You know what we want," Christopher says.

"Is that what this whole ruse with Grayson was about? He doesn't exist, does he?"

Christopher tilts his head and gives me a smirk.

"He does. Derek did lose his case and he was pissed. But he was on that flight and he was never after you."

I glare at him.

"Surprised you fell for it for as long as you did."

"So what? It was the two of you? You killed Derek and Susannah?"

"We don't need to go into all of that." He smiles a little at the corners of his lips.

"But you were defending me," I say. "Why were you even bothering to do that?"

"The cops had nothing on you."

"Yeah, because I had nothing to do with this."

"You needed a good defense," Christopher says. "Sandra was going to railroad you, and we already had more casualties than we needed to."

"What are you talking about?" I ask.

They exchange looks.

They don't have to say it. Susannah was an accident. She didn't have to be there.

"Susannah wasn't supposed to be there, was she?" I ask.

Shawn glares at Christopher.

"None of this had to happen the way that it did," Christopher says. "A lot of things happened that weren't supposed to, but it doesn't change the fact that we need that USB drive. We're not leaving here without it, and you, you can hand it over to us the nice way, or we'll have to do this the hard way."

"I don't know what you're talking about," I say. "You don't think that I would've wanted to turn this valuable piece of evidence over to my lawyer and my private investigator if I had it? I don't."

"Yeah, I think you do," Shawn says. "I think you do. And I think you know what's on it."

Cold sweat runs down my back.

I swallow hard.

"This house is big," Shawn says. "I've searched a lot of it, it's your turn. I'm going to take a little break."

The two of them leave me in the living room while they retreat to the kitchen to come up with a strategy. Still in a state of fog over what just happened, I tell myself to focus. I can think all of this over later. Now, I have to act.

Christopher and Shawn begin to argue. I overhear him talking about being worried about the cops coming around asking for me. Why are the cops looking for me?

Then I remember! I was going to meet up with Will and I stood him up. He's not looking for me in any official capacity. He's there just as a friend.

I look at the front door again.

Can I just go for it? Not with my hands tied to this. No.

I start picking at the wrapping around my wrists. It's tight but not tight enough.

There are a few loose spots and I go after them one at a time, loosening it just a little bit, as Christopher and Shawn continue to talk.

"We have to get rid of her," Christopher says. It's right out of earshot and Shawn shakes his head.

For a second I'm not sure if I heard him right. Why? Why would he say that?

"You started all this, Shawn. You have to finish it. We have to make sure she doesn't have the USB."

"She doesn't know where it is," Shawn says.

"I'm not so sure. Let me go look for it. You do, too," Christopher instructs. "But if we find nothing, we've got to make her talk and then..." He lets his voice drop off.

My hands and fingers go numb but I continue to work. The binding starts to loosen until it finally gives but I don't pull it off right away.

I wait for a few moments. Just as Christopher buries his head in one of the built-in cabinets underneath the television and Shawn starts to pull the refrigerator away from the wall, I make a run for it.

I had opened the sliding door to the backyard early this morning. I grab it, slide it to the left, and dash straight for the gate.

50

CHARLOTTE

When I pull up to Erin Lowry's house, I see Will's car at the corner.

He told me not to come but there was panic in his voice and I'm his partner. If they're going to take us off this case, I'm going to do my best to protect him and to find out who did it.

Just as I'm about to exit the vehicle, putting my phone in my back pocket, I see Erin Lowry exiting through the back gate and running across the lawn.

“Help!" she yells. "They're after me."

I pull out my weapon. One man I don't recognize runs after her. She looks back frightened and then heads toward me.

“Police!" I identify myself, yelling in his direction.

“Stop running! Police!”

But he continues to run.

A shot rings by my head. I duck down.

It's coming from somewhere else. There's another assailant.

I hide behind my vehicle, crouching down but pointing the gun in the first one's direction.

Another shot goes off. I spot Will behind his car, wincing in pain. He's been shot.

The first assailant takes off.

I shoot in his direction, but he's too experienced. He ducks behind a tree, then a car and a truck.

The assailant who is still in the house is helping him escape. When I try to shoot at the first guy's tires and peek out slightly from behind my vehicle for a better shot, the second one shoots at me, nearly hitting my shoulder.

As he speeds off, I study his license plate number to memorize it.

Erin is panting next to me, taking cover behind my vehicle.

"You okay?" I ask.

She nods, her teeth chattering. She rubs her wrists, I can tell that she'd been tied up. There's some bruising. All of this transpires in a matter of seconds.

"Who was there?" I say. "Who's in the house?"

"Christopher Flynn," she whispers. "My lawyer."

I don't have time to ask questions, so I rely on my training to respond.

"Christopher!" I yell, using my loud police announcer voice. "Christopher Flynn! Backup is coming. You're surrounded. You better come out now!"

"Who's the other guy?" I ask Erin. "The one who got away?"

"Shawn Nieves. My private investigator. They're working together. They're looking for some USB drive that they think I have," she starts to say but I lift up my hand to be quiet.

Will winces. He slouches behind his car, cradling his shoulder. When I try to go between the two vehicles, a shot rings out and I jump back.

I need to decide what to do. Do I stay here to deal with Christopher and let Shawn go?

I have Shawn's license plate number memorized and a few cops will be a lot more effective at tracking him down than I will, but what if he switches vehicles? We could lose him forever.

But I can't leave Will. Not in this state, with that maniac over there willing to kill everyone to get out of this.

“Where did he get that gun?” I ask Erin. “Did he stash it at your place?”

“I tried to escape once and I ran into him. He had a big duffel bag with him. I think he came with it.”

I look back at the house. It has been quiet for a few minutes and I wonder if Christopher has made an escape by jumping from Erin’s backyard to another.

"Let's go in," Will says, reading my mind. “You can go one way and I’ll go another so we can surround him in the yard."

"What about your shoulder?” I ask.

"It hurts, but I'll live. It just grazed it. You stay where you are.”

The amount of blood that has soaked into his shirt makes that unlikely but Will is tough.

Suddenly, Erin makes a run for it, trying to go from behind my car to Will’s. Another shot rings out, nearly hitting her. I’m pretty certain now that Christopher has a scope.

“What do you think you’re doing?” I snap. “You’re going to get yourself killed!”

"Christopher, come out!" Erin yells. "It's all over. They know that it's you and Shawn."

"They made up this whole thing about Thomas Grayson and how he was after me. And they framed me for what they did to Derek and Susannah."

She is speaking loud enough for Christopher to hear.

"What do you mean?" I ask.

"They killed them because there's some USB drive that Derek had, and he refused to give up. Then they thought that Derek had sent it to me or stashed it at my house. When they realized that they couldn't get it from me by making up the story about this Thomas Grayson boogeyman, they came straight out and threatened me, kept me in there, tied up. They were looking for it. They were going to torture me to make me talk. And clearly they're willing to kill for it."

"None of that is true!" Christopher yells from behind the house. "I am just trying to protect you."

"Is that why you held me hostage?" she yells back. "Is that why you tied me up?"

"Grayson needs that USB, otherwise you're dead."

I look around trying to decide what to do. Christopher's back is against the house and he has a rifle with a scope. So far he hasn't been a good shot, but that doesn't mean that he won't get lucky.

"I was trying to help you, Erin!" Christopher yells.

But his voice sounds slightly further away this time. I lean over for a closer look.

Is he making a run for it? When I lean over the hood of the car, I no longer see his shadow on the concrete walkway.

"I can't let him get away," I say, running toward the house.

"Where are you going?" Erin yells after me, blowing my cover.

"Shut up." Will pulls her down but I'm afraid it's too late and Christopher has heard her.

When I open the gate to the backyard, I see him scaling the wall to the neighbor.

I rush across the grass and jump up and over it. He shoots at me again, using a handgun this time, and I fall onto the grass for cover.

"Drop your weapon!" I warn as I position my Glock pistol in my right hand and stabilize with the left.

"Go to hell!" Christopher yells, shooting in my direction again.

A bullet flies over my head.

My ears start to buzz.

My heart is beating out of my chest. But I use every bit of my energy to concentrate.

Just as another bullet hits the ground next to me, I shoot.

I hit the calf of his left leg. He falls onto the ground in pain.

I take a moment to collect my thoughts. This is against protocol. He shot at me, I'm supposed to shoot to kill. But this case has so many unanswered questions that I'm not sure that justice will be served this way.

A moment later, Christopher grabs his weapon and starts to point it at me. I shoot again.

51

CHARLOTTE

Vehicles arrive, their sirens blaring. Everything starts to move in slow motion. It's almost like I'm watching the scene unfold on the screen instead of it happening to me.

I give my statement with Christopher's body still lying there, slumped over. I tell the deputies about the other assailant and give them the number of his license plate.

They put out an All-Points Bulletin for all law enforcement in the state to be on the lookout for his car. If Shawn is still in that car, they're going to find him.

I pull Erin aside and take her statement while Will gets treated in the ambulance. The shot went through the side of his shoulder, but didn't hit any vital organs.

Shaken and dazed, Erin goes through all the details of the day and being tied up while they searched the house without much success. She tells us about Christopher and Shawn pointing guns in her face and the ruse they put together about Thomas Grayson.

"Wasn't the private investigator somebody that your previous attorney recommended?" I ask.

"Yeah, but Christopher knew him as well from back in the day. He did a lot of work for Derek's firm and I think he was the only PI that Sandra knew."

Later that evening, two sheriff's deputies pull Shawn's car over about five hours from here. They know that he's armed and dangerous. Still, he doesn't go down without a fight. Shawn kills the first one, gravely injuring the other, but not before being shot dead by the second one.

The following morning, I meet with Will to see how he's doing.

"There will be a lot of recovery time, but it should be fine," he insists, nodding toward his sling.

We try not to discuss the day before, but what else is there to talk about?

"Both Christopher and Shawn are dead plus the deputy," I say. "Hopefully the other one will pull through."

I make a pot of coffee while Will sits at the kitchen table in his pajamas.

"But there's something I still don't understand," he says when I bring over two cups.

"What were they looking for? Was the USB ever there? Did she ever have it?"

"I have no idea," I say. "Erin says she has never heard of it or seen it, but you would know better than I would if she is telling the truth."

“If she says that she doesn’t know, I believe her. She has been honest about everything else,” Will says. “What do you think was on it?"

I shake my head and shrug, taking a long sip of my coffee.

"So how did this all happen?" Will asks.

"Christopher hired Shawn to kill his partner, Derek. We found it in his cleverly but not too disguised records. He billed Shawn’s fee to the firm if you can believe it, as a security consultant fee. It was just supposed be Derek that night, and he was just supposed to shoot him. But Susannah ended up canceling her trip to visit her mother, and she was there. He shot him and then shot her, too."

"What about all that blood?" Will asks. "All that blood that Erin fell in."

"He shot Susannah, but not well enough. I guess he thought that he killed her, but she was bleeding out for a while. Not sure whose idea it was, but they had it set up so that Erin would find her. She had been stalking them, anyway. She was the perfect fall guy."

"So then why would Christopher offer to represent her?" Will asks. "Because he wanted an in. He wanted to have all the inside information from the police. Since he didn't get along with Sandra, it only made sense he would be the inside guy."

"He probably wanted to get her convicted," Will says. "Maybe he took the case to make sure it happened."

"Yes, that's what I suspect, too," I say. "But then he realized that they didn't have this USB drive. They didn't know where it was. They looked everywhere. When Erin was getting close to getting arrested, Christopher realized that he needed her to talk to him and trust him even more. So they made up Grayson as a threat."

"What about the text?" Will asks.

"I think he sent it on purpose. I think he was following her and he saw that she was with Sandra, and then he'd have corroboration. That there's somebody after her. He honestly thought that she would give up the file if she had it. Maybe he thought that she would give up the file to try to protect Grayson, to try to get away from him. And that would be it. They would all be scot-free."

"But the file was never found?" he asks.

"Not yet."

52

ERIN

About a month after everything happened, I meet with Sandra for lunch and she offers me a job at her firm, associate, not junior associate with good pay, and lots of hours. They just took on a new client who is expanding their grocery store chain, and the work involved is expansive and full of billable hours.

"We need extra help," Sandra says, "and I know that it's something that will be a good fit for you."

"Thank you," I say. "I'd love to."

“The hours are going to be long though. I have to warn you.”

"It's fine," I say. I need something to occupy my mind after everything. I'm done moaning and doing nothing, wasting my life on the past.

We have a wonderful lunch and with each passing day, I start to feel more and more normal and believe more and more that perhaps after all of this and everything that has happened, I can rebuild my life.

I know that she's probably doing this because she feels guilty about being the one to hire Shawn and get me involved with him. But I promise her that given their plan, he would have been in my life no matter what. She was just a pawn and she has nothing to be sorry for.

Floating on cloud nine and excited for the future, I decide to stop for gas before popping into Trader Joe's for my weekly grocery shopping.

The gas tank cap is on a little too tight and I struggle with it for a few seconds before it finally breaks loose. The force sends it out of my hand in the opposite direction and it swings hard against the outside of the car.

Not thinking anything of it, I fill up the tank, but when I try to put the cap back on, it doesn't quite fit.

The seal got broken.

I try to fix the seal and force it harder, all to no avail. With each effort, it seems to break a little more.

It must be the mechanism, I say to myself, but how does it fit back on? I turn the flashlight on my phone on and shine it inside.

There, tucked in between the casing, I see a thin piece of plastic. When I shake the cap, it falls into my hand.

It's a slim USB drive.

WITH MY EARS clogged and my heart pounding loudly in my chest, I drive home grasping onto the USB so tightly that I worry that it might split in half.

“Relax. Take deep breaths,” I say to myself.

As soon as I walk through the door, I grab my laptop and stick the USB into the side. The first file I click on is a video.

It's Derek talking straight to the camera. He's sitting in his office at work. His pupils are dilated. His hair is frazzled and there’s a tumbler of scotch next to him on his mahogany table.

“I'm making this video on December 18th, 2021. I'm doing this because I feel like my life is in danger. I don't know when or where, but they're after me. I don't have any proof and I can't go to the police because I've done a lot of bad things as well.

Christopher Flynn joined the firm a number of years ago and he turned its trajectory. We started taking on clients that we shouldn't have, and I'll be the first to admit that I was lured in by the money as much as anyone else. But at some point, it got to be too much.

One day, I came in his office to print something out when my printer wasn't working and I saw the transfers from the firm account to various client accounts, as well as certain unmarked accounts in the Cayman Islands and elsewhere.

All of that information is contained here on this USB. I'm including it. All of our misdeeds, mine as well.

I should have said something earlier, but I didn't."

After taking a deep breath, he inhales a big gulp of the scotch. His hand shakes as he puts the glass back down on the table.

"Christopher didn't just embezzle money from the firm and the clients," Derek says, looking straight into the camera. "He also represented members of a cartel who were on trial for murder associated with their various drug businesses. He wasn't just their attorney. He helped them run their illegal empire. He covered up for them and he was even involved in the death of a police officer who was shot by the members of the cartel, operating in the valley. You will find more evidence of that here as well."

Derek pauses for a moment and looks away from the camera.

"A couple of months ago, I told him that I no longer wanted to be involved with anything so shady.

I wanted out. I have a new family, a baby on the way, and the money wasn't worth it, but I couldn't exactly leave. I knew too much and I started getting threats.

I was supposed to cooperate and I did to a degree, but the threats continued. I don't know who's after me, whether it's the cartel or the person that Christopher paid off or he himself and I don't know who's going to do it.

I hope it will blow over and I'm just being paranoid, but I'm making this recording to explain everything.

I'm not sure who to trust, except my ex-wife who always believed me when she shouldn't have and who deserves much more than a scumbag like me."

I pause the video and I click through the rest of the materials in the file and find a plethora of evidence about everything that he mentions. My hand shakes and tears well up in my eyes. Derek was almost out of this. They didn't have to die, but one thing still lingers in my mind.

How was he going to get this to me? What was the plan?

I turn the video back on.

"I'm going to hide this file in the gas tank of her car. Then I will message or email her and tell her what she needs to do, without any other explanation. I think this will keep Erin safe, at least I hope so."

I stare into Derek's face. After all that, he still trusted me. I'm not so happy that he got me involved, but he thought highly of me and I appreciate that, as well as the apology.

But that text, that email never came. Why not?

This video was made just ten days before his death and that means that he put it there, but didn't have the chance to contact me.

So if they hadn't come looking for it, I would've never found it and their plan would've worked.

I was stalking his house, following him everywhere. I was an easy target. Why not slip something in my drink, wait until I wake up a little bit, and point me toward his house?

53

CHARLOTTE

The day before his first day back, I stop by for a surprise visit during a lull on my morning shift. Even though he just woke up, Will looks good. He has nice color back in his face and an attitude to match.

He invites me in and we chat for a little while about anything and everything except Erin. I don't know if it's right for me to keep his secret, but I'm a loyal friend.

"I don't know if you're going to tell the department about you and Erin now that everything has blown over, but, if you do, I want you to warn me first. I need a head's up," I say.

"I wasn't planning on it. I figured let's leave well enough alone. If they don't already know, maybe they never will."

"Yeah. Maybe not," I agree despite thinking that secrets tend to not stay hidden forever.

"So I'm heading out to Long Beach this weekend," I tell him. "Got invited to a reunion."

"How many years has it been?"

"Twenty. It's a middle school reunion, a bit unorthodox. But I lived there for three years, so it made an impact," I say with a tinge of sarcasm and a smile.

"Well, I hope you have a good time."

I nod.

"It's going to be nice to see all those people again. Catch up on everything that's happened. Reminisce about the past. Do you have anything you want to keep to yourself from that time?" Will jokes. "If you do, it's bound to come out, you know."

He smiles and gives me a wink and a cold sweat runs down the side of my body.

He doesn't know anything about what happened then. I do and perhaps going back is kicking a hornet's nest. But what happened shouldn't have stayed a secret for so long.

"Detective Pierce, I'm sorry. I had no idea you were here." Erin comes out dressed in a bathrobe. Her hair is tossed and she's clearly spent the night.

Will looks away.

"I know that the case is over," I whisper. "But you *can't* have a relationship with her."

"Why?" Will asks.

"You *know* why. It's dangerous. If anyone were to find out—"

"Erin had nothing to do with their murders," Will interrupts me.

"I know, but it can look like she was proven innocent due to your involvement with her."

Erin walks out, leaving us alone.

"Charlotte, promise that you won't say a word."

I look him straight in the eyes.

"Of course. But your career will suffer if anyone else were to ever uncover this secret. You will probably get fired."

I promise not to say anything, just like I had promised not to say anything before.

But secrets have a way of coming out at the most inconvenient time. I thought that this thing that happened would remain hidden forever.

Yet here it is, making waves somewhere deep below.

I get back into my car and stare at the invitation.

Do I stay or do I go?

THANK YOU FOR READING! I hope you enjoyed the first Detective Charlotte Pierce novel. Cant' wait to read more? Dive into **WHEN SHE LEFT now**!

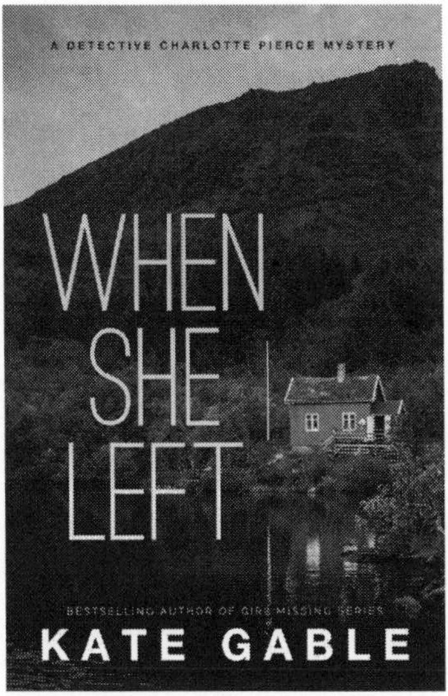

When a 13-year-old girl vanished, her friends have kept certain details of that night a secret. Even though she was only a teenager, this mistake continues to haunt Detective Charlotte Pierce.

Twenty years later, Charlotte attends her middle school reunion and begins to investigate what happened to her friend that night.

Meanwhile, back home in Mesquite County, CA, another **teenager reports her sister missing and comes home to discover that both of her parents have been brutally murdered**.

Will Charlotte be able to locate the missing girl and find out who killed her parents and why?

Will Charlotte ever find out that truth about what happened to her friend that night?

1-Click WHEN SHE LEFT now!

IF YOU ENJOYED THIS BOOK, please take a moment to write a short review on your favorite book site and maybe recommend it to a friend or two.

DON'T WANT to wait until the new release and want to dive into another series right now? Make sure to grab **GIRL HIDDEN (a novella) for FREE!**

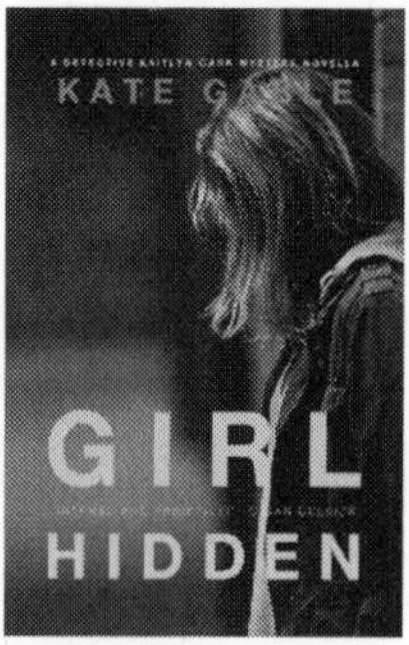

A family is found dead in their home. The only survivor is the teenage daughter who managed to escape the burning house.

Who killed them? And why? **Detective Kaitlyn Carr has to bring their killer to justice.**

A year before her disappearance, Violet, Kaitlyn's sister, comes to stay with her after a bad fight with their mom.

She can't stand living at home as much as Kaitlyn once did and wants to move in with her.

What happens when the dysfunction of her own family threatens to blow up her face and let the killer off for good?

GRAB GIRL HIDDEN for FREE now!

If you enjoyed this book, please take a moment to write a short review on your favorite book site and maybe recommend it to a friend or two.

You can also join my Facebook group, Kate Gable's Reader Club, for exclusive giveaways and sneak peeks of future books.

BE THE FIRST TO KNOW ABOUT MY UPCOMING SALES, NEW RELEASES AND EXCLUSIVE GIVEAWAYS!

Want a Free book? Sign up for my Newsletter!

Sign up for my newsletter:
https://www.subscribepage.com/kategableviplist

Join my Facebook Group:
https://www.facebook.com/groups/833851020557518

Bonus Points: Follow me on BookBub and Goodreads!

https://www.goodreads.com/author/show/21534224.Kate_Gable

ABOUT KATE GABLE

Kate Gable loves a good mystery that is full of suspense. She grew up devouring psychological thrillers and crime novels as well as movies, tv shows and true crime.

Her favorite stories are the ones that are centered on families with lots of secrets and lies as well as many twists and turns. Her novels have elements of psychological suspense, thriller, mystery and romance.

Kate Gable lives near Palm Springs, CA with her husband, son, a dog and a cat. She has spent more than twenty years in Southern California and finds inspiration from its cities, canyons, deserts, and small mountain towns.

She graduated from University of Southern California with a Bachelor's degree in Mathematics. After pursuing graduate studies in mathematics, she switched gears and got her MA in Creative Writing and English from Western New Mexico University and her PhD in Education from Old Dominion University.

Writing has always been her passion and obsession. Kate is also a USA Today Bestselling author of romantic suspense under another pen name.

Write her here:

Kate@kategable.com

Check out her books here:

www.kategable.com

Sign up for my newsletter:
https://www.subscribepage.com/kategableviplist

Join my Facebook Group:
https://www.facebook.com/groups/833851020557518

Bonus Points: Follow me on BookBub and Goodreads!

https://www.bookbub.com/authors/kate-gable

https://www.goodreads.com/author/show/21534224.Kate_Gable

amazon.com/Kate-Gable/e/B095XFCLL7
facebook.com/kategablebooks
bookbub.com/authors/kate-gable
instagram.com/kategablebooks

ALSO BY KATE GABLE

All books are available at ALL major retailers! If you can't find it, please email me at **kate@kategable.com**

Detective Kaitlyn Carr

Girl Missing (Book 1)
Girl Lost (Book 2)
Girl Found (Book 3)
Girl Taken (Book 4)
Girl Forgotten (Book 5)
Girl Hidden (FREE Novella)

Detective Charlotte Pierce

What She Did
When She Left
How She Disappeared

Made in the USA
Middletown, DE
05 April 2022

63673742R00234